HOW
TO ROB A
BANK

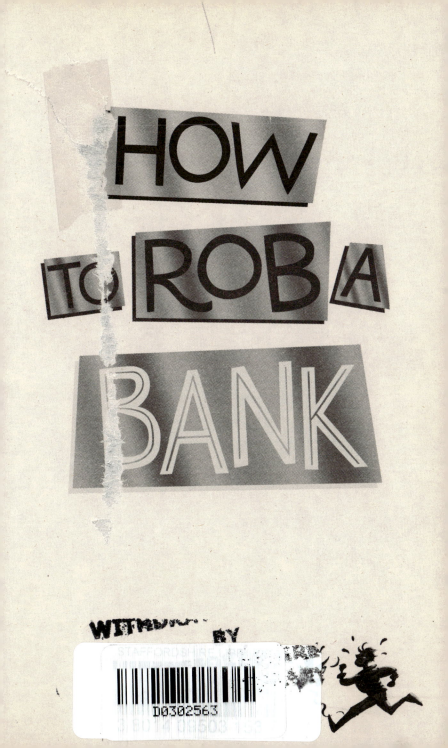

HOW TO ROB A BANK

TOM MITCHELL

HarperCollins *Children's Books*

First published in Great Britain by
HarperCollins *Children's Books* in 2019
HarperCollins *Children's Books* is a division of HarperCollins*Publishers* Ltd,
HarperCollins Publishers
1 London Bridge Street
London SE1 9GF

The HarperCollins website address is:
www.harpercollins.co.uk

4

ISBN 978–0–00–827650–8

Typeset in Plantin by
Palimpsest Book Production Ltd, Falkirk, Stirlingshire
Printed and bound by CPI Group (UK) Ltd, Croydon CR0 4YY

To Jacob, Dylan and Nicky

PART 1

CHAPTER 1

Identify Your Justification: Why Bother?

Ask yourself – do I need the money? Robbing a bank isn't something to do to pass the time, like kicking footballs over the neighbour's fence or reading. Some people rob banks because they're greedy. Those people are usually caught after buying muscle cars or diamond-encrusted baseball caps. Others enjoy the adrenalin rush of thrusting sawn-off shotguns into the faces of middle-aged women. Those are typically twenty-somethings with troubled childhoods.

Me? I robbed a bank because of guilt. Specifically: guilt and a Nepalese scented candle.

Let me explain.

It was an endless summer and I was fifteen and fed up with playing *Call of Duty* and *FIFA*. There are only so many times you can get sniped in the chin or spanked five–nil before you start questioning the meaning of it all. Mum and Dad's moaning meant I'd applied for part-time jobs. But even McDonald's had turned me down. Dad said this was evidence of Broken Britain. Mum said I shouldn't stop trying.

It was a Saturday afternoon, one of those boring summer Saturdays without Premier League football and with lasagne planned for dinner. Dad was on the sofa, Mum was on the wine, and Rita was on the phone. And all my friends, apart from Beth, were on exotic holidays with never-ending beaches and azure oceans.

'What do you know about Watergate and Richard Nixon?' asked Dad. His question, like most of his questions, was a run-up to convincing me to watch a film. This time, it was *All the President's Men*, which he'd first shown me when I was in primary school and I'd thought boring and confusing.

I told him I was off to see a girl. That shut him up.

'Good for you,' said Mum, who was at the dining table, holding a dog-eared magazine in one hand and a chipped wine glass in the other.

'Yes,' said Dad, waving a hand to silence Mum. 'Live a little.'

Dad was being ironic. It was something else he did – watching films and being ironic. That was Dad. Also – snoring.

I went to my room, closed the door, and ignored the smell of sweat that rose like shimmering heat waves from my stained duvet. I fell to my knees and ran my hands underneath the bed. My fingers passed over crisp packets and sticky patches that I'd worry about later. Finally I found the package I'd been searching for. It had been hiding here since Monday when Brian, our seven-foot-tall German postman, had stood at our front door and had said:

'Parcel for you. *Ist* party time?'

And he'd smiled a smile so bright that to look directly into his mouth would blind you.

TBH, I wasn't 100 per cent convinced a Nepalese scented candle would impress my friend Beth. But I'd cornered myself when Harry, a drippy guy in the year below, had asked what I'd got Beth for her birthday.

Beth lets Harry follow her around because their mums are members of the same yoga club or something. He thinks they're best friends but they're so not.

I didn't even know she had a birthday. I mean, I know everyone has a birthday but . . .

'I'm a teenager,' I said. 'I don't buy friends birthday presents. I don't even write on their Facebook walls.'

'I bought her a necklace,' said Harry. 'It's silver.'

Round Beth's neck was this pretty thing with tiny dolphins that I'd not noticed until now.

'Honestly,' said Beth, 'I don't care about presents.'

I confess: I panicked.

'A Nepalese scented candle,' I said. 'That's what I got you.'

And I said this because only the day before, Dad had watched me order Mum a Nepalese scented candle on the internet. It was her birthday soon and he thought it would be good for me to get her something that smelt nice.

'A Nepalese scented candle?' Beth said on the swings in the rec, swinging as only teenage girls can swing. 'That sounds cool.'

'It sounds lame,' said Harry.

I didn't take any notice of Harry because he said everything was lame.

So, days later, in my room, kneeling at my bed like I was praying to the god of smelly things you buy the women in your life, I thought, *Yeah, Dad, I will take a risk. I'll give Beth a Nepalese scented candle.*

Beth lived in a home built by her angry builder dad to resemble a miniature version of the White House and she looked exactly like Emma Stone. Like exactly. Like getting stopped in the street by old men exactly like Emma Stone. Google Emma Stone. That's what Beth looked like. Really.

Even though her home was a baby version of the White House, it was actually massive compared to everyone else's and especially mine. It even had its own cinema room, although the screen had yet to be installed. Her mum used the space to hang washing and it smelt of damp and regret.

I'd not told Dad about the cinema room. It might send him into a spiral of depression, whatever that means.

CHAPTER 2

Exercise Caution Around Naked Flames

Forty minutes after retrieving the package, I was sitting on Beth's bed and telling her to shut the door. If I acted assertively, I might forget I was in a girl's bedroom and all the associated confusing feelings like wanting to run but also to stay here forever. The curtains were still drawn from the night, but this was good. I nodded at the poster of Andrew Garfield. He was looking at a horse. I wondered how it would feel to fall asleep looking at Andrew Garfield looking at a horse. I wouldn't like it.

'I'd have tidied if I'd known you were coming,' she said, kicking clothes out of the way. I think I saw knickers.

Before anything, I asked, 'Where's Harry?'

'Coming,' she said. 'You know . . . he's either here or . . . he's coming here.'

I pulled the package out of my jeans. The padded envelope was bent and twisted. Lionel Messi looked down from alongside Andrew Garfield and I couldn't help thinking he stared at me as if I were an idiot. Still, he wasn't as good as he used to be.

'Happy birthday,' I said.

Beth joined me. The mattress sighed. I could feel her body radiating warmth. I handed over the package.

'Nice wrapping,' she said, studying the battered envelope.

She pulled the top off. Inside were strips of newspaper. She shook these out.

(What if there was nothing else inside and I ended up looking like an idiot? Again.)

The candle plopped to the floor like a calf from a cow. It was squat and circular like a stack of digestive biscuits. There was a shiny metal rim round the soapy-looking wax. In the centre, a black wick drooped.

'Thanks,' said Beth, her Emma Stone lips forming a smile.

Was it an impressed smile or a laughing-at-Dylan smile?

'A candle,' I said, picking it up.

9

'Nepalese scented?' she replied. 'You know, Mum sometimes runs a bath and lights these when she's had enough of Dad.'

'They're supposed to be therapeutic,' I said, guessing.

'You saying I'm stressed?'

'We're all stressed,' I said in a quiet voice.

I hoped she couldn't see my tell-tale heart quaking beneath the Crystal Palace replica shirt.

'Let's light it!' she said, bouncing up from the bed.

She crossed to her desk and pulled open the top drawer. There was a rush of pens and paper. Finally she found what she'd been looking for – a lighter. Did she smoke? She didn't smoke. She was Beth.

The lighter, cheap and plastic, turned cartwheels as it flew through the air and hit me squarely on the forehead. Beth laughed. I rubbed my head and asked if we were lighting it.

'Why not?'

'Your mum?'

'What about my mum?'

'She might think, you know, that we've been smoking or something?'

Now it wasn't only Messi who looked at me as if I were an idiot. I held the lighter and inspected the candle.

What if it smelt horrible? What if the scent had hallucinogenic properties and made us go crazy? People jump out of windows and all sorts.

I took the candle to Beth's desk and pushed away a pile of revision workbooks to make space. I flicked the lighter. It didn't catch. I flicked again. An orange flame erupted. I held it to the wick. It caught. A smell blossomed. A combination of wet dog and herbs.

I coughed, my shoulders jumping. The scent of the Nepalese scented candle was a real throat-tickler.

And, at this point, the heavy feet of Beth's mum began pounding towards us from the corridor.

'Mum!' hissed Beth. 'It stinks! Put it out! Get rid of it! It's not Nepalese!'

Now coughing too, she forced her back against the door and pointed desperately to the wastebin over-flowing with Coke cans and crisps that sat under the window.

I licked my fingers and pinched at the flame. I felt needle-sharp pain and, despite myself, let out a tiny yelp.

Beth's eyes almost exploded from their sockets.

I grabbed the still-smoking candle and threw it at the bin. Such was the horror of monster mother's footsteps getting louder, I didn't register the amazing shot. Bull's-eye. Next to go was the lighter. This hit the brim of the bin and fell behind, unseen. By now Beth's mum was knocking at the door. I yanked open the window and flapped my hands while scanning the room for deodorant to spray to cover the stink.

'Just a second,' shouted Beth. 'I'm not decent.'

There! Under the desk! A pink aerosol can!

'Not decent? Haven't you got Dylan in there, young lady?' her mum asked.

Beth stepped forward and the door opened, striking the back of her head.

'Ow!'

I sprayed a feeble burst of aerosol as Beth rubbed her head. And Beth's mum took in the full vision of the darkened room and she wasn't impressed.

My cheeks burnt red.

'What's going on?' she asked, eyeing the strange pile of newspaper strips. 'And why does it smell of yoga in here?'

'Hello, Mrs Fraser,' I said. 'How are you?'

My voice wavered. Beth's mum looked like Emma Stone in her mid-forties. Emma Stone in her mid-forties narrowing her eyes.

'Dylan Thomas,' she said. 'Are you writing any poetry yet?'

'Not yet,' I said.

She nodded.

'Why are you holding Beth's deodorant?'

I had nothing to say. I looked to Beth. She looked at me.

'Muuuum,' she said after a while.

'I was sweaty?' I offered.

Her mum's eyes narrowed further, a slit of iris remaining, until –

'You two! I'm not angry! I understand.' She grinned. 'I was young once . . . if you can believe that.'

My cheeks exploded in embarrassment. Beth mumbled something unintelligible and I couldn't help noticing how she scrunched up her nose in disgust.

'I've got Pringles downstairs,' Mrs Fraser said.

With her hand on the doorknob, she stood back to allow us through. Neither of us looked at the bin as we passed.

We were sitting at the dining table, eating Pringles, drinking Coke and listening to Mrs Fraser tell us how important getting a good set of GCSEs is when we first saw the dark mass of smoke spread its tendrils down from the staircase to the carpet. Mrs Fraser, with her back to the stairs, thought Beth was joking when she stood and pointed and shouted 'Look!'

'Never mind all that,' Mrs Fraser said. 'I want to know how you plan to pass English when you never do any reading.'

Like someone had started a bonfire on the stairs, the same thick, earthy clouds of smoke blossomed towards us.

'Oh my days,' I said when I saw what Beth was pointing at.

The dark smoke moved silently and stealthily like dry ice at a school musical. There was something unreal and uncanny about the way it thickened into the space.

When Mrs Fraser saw it she screamed, 'Don't panic!'

She ushered us from the room and out of the house, panicking and shouting, 'The White House is on fire! The White House is on fire! Don't panic! Don't panic!'

Outside, stood Harry. We rushed past as he pointed at the smoke spilling from the front door and whispered in awe, 'So not lame.'

In 1814, British soldiers burnt down the White House. It must have looked like this. But bigger. And with fewer Nissan Qashqais parked outside.

That very afternoon, Beth's house, Pringles, scented candle, posters of Andrew Garfield, Lionel Messi and all, burnt away to nothing but ashes and twisted metal. The destruction was complete.

And my thumb and forefinger hurt for days.

CHAPTER 3

Remember: There's No 'I' in 'Team' But There is in 'Win'

A few days after the fire, I saw Beth walking through the rec with a thick black sports bag over her shoulder. Harry trailed close behind, pulling a grey wheeled suitcase. It bounced across the uneven turf. He raised two fingers at me. I didn't know where they were going or where they'd been.

I'd called out. 'Do you want a hand?'

I wanted to say more, to apologise to Beth, but didn't know which words to use. They all seemed wrong. And I had no idea how much Harry knew. I didn't want to mug myself off.

'Sorry for burning down your house, yo!' would be a stupid thing to shout, however much I wanted to.

Beth stopped. She smiled as if a dentist had asked her to show off her gums, i.e. not very convincingly.

'Really?' I called, jogging to catch up.

'It's all good,' she said. 'We're in a sweet flat with views across London.'

Harry stood at her shoulder, nodding like a broken doll.

Her home, the burnt one, had gone viral. Images of the tiny, fiery White House had swept through Twitter, with jokes about Trump and everything.

'Tell him about your stuff,' said Harry.

He'd swapped his nodding for a pulling-legs-off-a-spider grin.

'It's nothing,' said Beth.

She dropped the sports bag. It wheezed as it hit the grass.

'What about your stuff? Did you manage to save anything?'

Beth squinted but it may have been because of the sun. And the water in her eyes was probably due to hay fever too. Not that she ever got hay fever.

'No,' she said. 'It's all gone. My clothes. My books. My stuff. But, you know, someone said your possessions end up possessing you, so . . .'

Her voice tailed off. I felt that churning in my stomach, a Vindaloo guilt like I'd eaten a secret curry the night before.

'At least you've got your phone,' I said, because of all the things to lose, your phone's got to be the worst.

'Yeah,' said Harry. 'At least you've got your phone, Beth. Everything else is up in smoke, but you can still Instagram.'

Beth shushed Harry. Not only did it stop him talking but it also stopped him smiling.

'It'll be fine,' I said because that's what you say when bad things have happened. 'Your mum and dad will work something out.'

(They had money, after all.)

'Yeah,' said Beth. 'And it's sunny out and the end of the summer is, like, weeks away and we've got sick views and I can always buy new clothes, so . . .'

But her heart wasn't in her words.

I watched them fade from the rec, a panting Harry following like a squire to his knight. Why'd I mention her phone? How was that any help? The word on the street was that faulty wiring was the cause of the fire but *my* scented candle had so burnt down Beth's house. I mean, the wick was still smoking when I'd thrown it in the bin.

It *was* the cause of the fire, for sure. So sure that I'd spent the time between being picked up from the blazing home (a crowd had formed outside pointing at the flames licking up from the windows) and seeing Beth in the park expecting a knock at the door from the police or, worse, Beth's angry dad. I couldn't sleep. I couldn't even focus on *Football Manager*.

I'd destroyed Beth's house and everything in it.

(But if she'd lost all her possessions, what was in the bags? I *bet* Harry was sucking up and, like, offering to lend her towels and all sorts.)

CHAPTER 4

Does Robbing a Bank Suit Your Needs?

On the way home from the rec I stopped at the corner shop to buy a Lion Bar in the desperate hope that sugar would make things better. I told myself the whole faulty wiring thing was reason to be happy, even if it weren't true. *It's a post-fact world*, I thought. I still felt supernova guilty, but at least I wasn't going to prison. Prison would be bad for a boy of my imagination and size. And, anyway, houses have insurance, Mum said, and Beth's family would be able to claim expensive things had been destroyed, so—

'It's not all bad,' Mum had said last night, sipping wine. 'Remember the time we were broken into and you claimed for a Blu-ray, Kay?'

Dad did not remember.

'Must have been another husband,' he'd said from the sofa.

Stepping from the corner shop, my world focused on unwrapping the Lion Bar, I heard a voice.

'Buy us a . . .' it began.

It was a voice wavering from high to low, a voice unsure whether to commit to adulthood. It was Dave's voice. Dave Royston. The biggest melt in the neighbourhood. He hung about on the corner, smoking cigarettes and thinking he was a gangster. His cronies, Adam and Ben, like gophers on alert, stood at either shoulder. I don't think I'd ever heard Adam or Ben speak, only their high-pitched laughter like hyenas on helium.

I took a bite from the Lion Bar. If I should die, it wouldn't be on an empty stomach.

It tasted of heaven and caramel.

'Dylan!' he said. 'You muppet! What you doing? Buying poetry?'

I stepped to the side. He did the same to stop me passing.

'No,' I said quietly, chewing. 'They don't sell poetry here.'

'Give us your Lion Bar. Nobody eats chocolate on this corner without my say.'

He snatched the Lion Bar from my hand. I couldn't be bothered to do anything about it, only hoping there was a terrible disease in my saliva that would make his testicles fall off. He took a bite and chewed with his mouth open. His privates weren't obviously affected.

'Just saw your girlfriend. In the rec. High-rise Beth. Shame. I thought they were loaded.'

'What?'

Dave laughed and it sounded like a theremin.

'You don't know? Her, her mum, her dad, all moving to a tiny flat in one of the high-rises. Serves her right. Llama's a bitch.'

'Karma,' I said, dropping a shoulder left, then moving right. My winger's feint deceived Dave and I pushed past Ben.

The high-rise? That couldn't be right. Beth's family had money. They had a cinema room, even though the screen had yet to be fitted and it had burnt down. The high-rises towered over the east of town like huge, broken teeth. She couldn't be living there. No way. She looked like a movie star, I mean, and she'd said they'd moved somewhere with a nice view. She couldn't have meant there.

If this had been a film, I might have fallen to my knees and lifted my fists to the sky and shouted 'Noooo!'

What had I done?

Dad's van, white and with *Thomas and Son, Plumbers etc.* on the side, was parked outside our house.

Dad was in the front room.

'I came home early to spend time with my favourite son. Where've you been? What d'you want to do?'

I told Dad I didn't want to do anything. I told him I'd bumped into Beth. I told him I had a headache. Dad's tone changed gears, shifting down to compassion.

'What was she up to?'

'Walking. Probably to the high-rise. Because an idiot burnt down her house.'

Dad's eyes grew warm. He stretched a hand to my shoulder. It didn't reach.

'That's a lesson about insurance,' he said. 'You've heard they had no insurance, right? You've got to have insurance. We live in an insured world. Just goes to show, doesn't it? Remember this, son. Insurance.'

How did everyone know everything but me? I should check Facebook more often.

I later found out, on Facebook, that Beth's dad wasn't

23

a successful builder after all. He'd spent the family's money, inherited, building the house I'd destroyed. He'd planned to sell it at a profit, but it turned out nobody wanted to live in a mini version of the White House, not in England anyway. So the family occupied the building as Beth's dad continued to lower and lower the asking price, until –

'Do *we* have insurance?' I asked.

Dad smiled. 'We do now.'

I felt the weight of the high-rise across my shoulders. I couldn't forget Beth's face as she trudged across the rec. Like your favourite teacher, not angry but disappointed. A deflated Emma Stone. And all because of me.

'Shall we watch a film?' I said.

At least I could make *him* happy.

Dad knew just the thing, he always does: something to take our minds off fires and insurance. He'd recorded it the night before and although it was full of swearwords and violence, it was a straight-up classic. Something I needed to watch for sure.

'Your English teacher can bang on about Shakespeare and Wordsworth as much as she likes,' he said. 'But some films are as important a part of your education.'

'What's it called?' I asked, settling into the sofa next

to his warmth. He was still in the bleach-blanched tracksuit bottoms that he'd worn to work. At least he'd taken his boiler suit off. '*Dog Day Afternoon*. It's based on a true story. I know they all say that, but this one really is. You won't believe it, but it's true. And it has Al Pacino before he became a diva.'

We watched the film. And that afternoon, and for the first time ever, Dad changed my life.

Dog Day Afternoon: definitely in my top-ten bank robbery films, maybe even top five. And especially important for being the film that decided how I'd make everything better:

BANK ROBBERY.

I'd rob a bank and I'd make good. I wasn't sure how much money nice houses cost or suburban banks held, but at the very least we could go shopping and replace all Beth's stuff. And maybe even pay for her to live somewhere nicer than the high-rise. I'd probably still have enough left over to buy a sports car (and a chauffeur to drive it) and there'd be cash too for Dad to stop work for six months and write the screenplay he always said he had in him when he'd drunk too much. Mum could buy a share in a vineyard or something. I wouldn't give any money to Rita because she didn't deserve it.

So long, History coursework and your 'Why did the USA become involved in Vietnam in the 1950s and 1960s?' (30 marks). Hello, master criminal and 'What's the most effective way of robbing a bank?' (£1,000,000).

Best get Googling.

CHAPTER 5

There's Such a Thing as Being Over-prepared

As with any skilled occupation, robbing a bank requires specialist equipment. The type of specialist equipment not easily obtained by fifteen-year-olds. Specialist equipment like guns, for example. In the night following *Dog Day Afternoon*, I lay in bed and my blind eyes stared through the darkness and I felt guilty and I thought about stuff.

I thought about using a stun gun. Obviously an actual gun was a non-starter. I mean, I'm an idiot but not that much of an idiot. Could you convince a bank worker to hand over cash in exchange for not being Tasered? And was I mean enough to do that?

I was pretty sure you could buy one online. Not Amazon (unless you lived in the States) but from a dodgier part of the internet: the place Palace buy their centre backs, the dark Web. It's like Amazon but with illegal stuff and a slightly higher chance of getting arrested.

Getting a stun gun delivered to your own house would be a mistake of course, but as Dave Royston lived round the corner I'd just use his address. It would be amateur-level easy to intercept Brian the German postman or somehow get to the package before Dave, which is exactly what I did two years ago when buying bangers off eBay (fireworks, not sausages). And if it all went wrong? Well, Dave saw himself as a gangster. He'd get his mugshot on the news and everything. I could just imagine the scene . . .

The suburban road, all drawn curtains and tired trees, quiet except for the slam of car doors as commuters climbed into Ford Fiestas and Nissan Micras. Suddenly the roar of sirens would break that silence as police transit vans pulled up outside Dave's house. People dressed like video-game police would pour out of the vans, their guns bouncing against their chests as they thrust forward, up the crazy paving of Dave's front path. The SWAT team would rush Dave's door and, the next thing you know, Dave is face down on the tarmac with the lead SWAT guy telling him, 'No one moves around here without my say-so.'

Would I feel sorry for Dave if he were arrested because of a stun gun I'd ordered? Probably not. He *had* stolen my Lion Bar.

Still, as much as all this would be funny, the sad truth is that only idiots rob banks with guns, even stun guns. I'd done the research like I'd planned my History coursework. On my iPhone, in the toilet, I'd googled 'armed robbery'. I'd discovered the moment you take a gun to the party, even if it's a stun gun, the sentences imposed by judges jump higher than a frog full of helium. And the truth is I wouldn't feel great waving guns around, even if the worse they could do was stun.

The room was thick with steam and thinking. And was a bit stinky TBH.

I don't need a Taser, I thought. No. I'd use a better weapon to hold up a bank: MY BRAIN!

(But not literally. You know what I mean.)

In *Out of Sight*, a 1998 film, George Clooney robs a bank using nothing. No accomplices, no guns, nothing. All he does is enter one of those air-conditioned Hollywood banks with old-style ringing phones and tidy desks and he spots a stranger chatting with a bank manager at some polite table. The stranger has a leather briefcase on the floor. Clooney approaches a teller (the

American who gives out the cash) and tells them he has an accomplice. He points at the stranger who, for all Clooney knows is chatting about the weather, and says the guy has a handgun in his briefcase and should Clooney give the signal, he'll pull it out and shoot the bank manager. Of course, it being George Clooney, the teller believes him and hands over an envelope bursting with dollars.

I'm no George Clooney, but, like Clooney, I'm able to walk and talk, most of the time anyway, and that's all it took for Clooney's character to rob the bank.

FYI Clooney eventually gets caught. How? His getaway car has a flat battery. As Mr Stones, the coach of the U13 football team used to say: 'Fail to prepare, prepare to fail.' Mr Stones didn't say much else, apart from 'It's the taking part that counts.'

CHAPTER 6

Ensure Your Target Ticks All the Boxes

Location, location, location. The fewer associations you have with your target, the better. Unlike George Clooney, I couldn't drive. And my parents would notice if I were off catching planes and trains. So, like at school, my geography was limited.

I went on Google Maps, centred my location, and searched for 'post office', thinking that a post office would possess less security than a bank. You normally get a Perspex screen and Google says there's usually a panic button under the counter but what you don't get are armed guards and drooling Rottweilers. What I had in mind was a *Postman Pat*-style set-up, with an elderly woman who sits next to a container of lollipops and knits all day. She'd call me 'sonny' and offer no physical objection to the robbery. I'd simply be another example of the rotten state of modern youth. Like Al Pacino says in *Dog Day Afternoon*, these places have insurance. Nobody would be losing out. Granny would have a new story for her bingo friends. Broken Britain. Who cares?

Outside, the rain fell without break from low clouds the colour of failure. Bad weather is a constant during school holidays. When we grow up and get jobs, we'll be sitting in our offices and it'll be sweltering outside, guaranteed. Global warming.

Dad was on the sofa watching a Western and scratching himself. He was meant to be unblocking the drain of a house belonging to the parents of a rich kid in the year above, but he couldn't do much when it was raining. He said this whenever there was the slightest suggestion of moisture in the air, whether the job was inside or out. Either way, it was a pretty lame excuse when you're a plumber and getting wet was pretty much first on the list of things you'd expect to happen during the working day.

'Want to join me?' he said, patting the cushions with the hand that had recently been down his jogging bottoms. 'It's only just started. Mum won't be back for ages. How's the job search going?'

After my half-hearted application to McDonald's, Mum and Dad had got it into their heads I was actually applying for jobs, and not only this but having a part-time summer job was, like, the best idea ever.

The edges of my mouth curled downwards. Crazy sounds like someone was breaking up furniture with a pig came from the TV. In a darkened bedroom, a man was hugging a woman. He was wearing a cowboy hat.

'We can fast-forward the rude bits,' Dad said, his hands searching for the remote controls as the cowboy grunted. 'It's violent and sweary. You'd like it. It's not all cuddles.' He paused. 'Like life really.'

Upstairs, Rita's movements rolled through the house like teenage thunder. And even though you could hear the rain drumming on the roof, I told Dad I had to go out.

'To do what?'

'Homework,' I said. I looked to the TV. 'With a girl. And then jobs. You know.'

The naughty cowboy meant I could leave without feeling guilty. Because I was only a kid. The film would corrupt my morals.

The front door was open as I shouted through to Dad, 'It's holiday coursework.'

'Wear a jacket,' said Dad, defeated by the c-word.

So, with the pre-prepared threatening note in my back pocket, I took a bus to the target, Krazy Prices. I found the old Arsenal shirt Nan had bought me for Xmas. At the time, Dad had said her confusion was a warning sign of dementia, but I honestly think she didn't know the difference between Palace and Arsenal.

'They both play in London, don't they?' she'd said, biting her false teeth into a mince pie. 'Don't be such a fusspot.'

They have CCTV on buses. They have CCTV everywhere, but they have it particularly on buses. If you're lucky, you might sit on one with its own display and get to stare at people without looking weird. They use these bus images for missing kids: Charlton teenager last seen on the 53. And there's a grainy black-and-white screen grab that could be anyone with a face, but looks like a ghost, which it kind of is.

My thinking – if the police were to bother searching the bus CCTV for the ballsy teenager who'd emptied a local post office of all its cash, they'd see a kid with an Arsenal shirt and a baseball cap, two things I never wear.

It took three goes with my Oyster but the driver had the *Daily Mail* open on her lap and didn't turn her head when I stepped on. The bus smelt of fried chicken. The bottom deck was full of mums with prams and grannies with wheeled shopping baskets, so I climbed upstairs.

I took a seat in the middle. Screwed into the ceiling above the front window was a black hemisphere. Through its glass you could just about make out a camera. I pulled down my cap and dug my chin into my chest. I thought about the post office. About the note. As long as I believed all would be fine, all *would* be fine.

Rain smudged the windows, bending the vague shapes of the outside world out of focus. I stared at nothing and tried to think positive thoughts.

The rain's intensity faded as the bus dropped me off only a few metres away from the post office. Krazy Prices looked to be a counter at the back of a corner shop. The *Guardian* sponsored its awning: a middle-class neighbourhood. I checked for the note in my back pocket, the key to today's successful robbery. After confirming it was there, I took a deep breath, which tightened my chest even more, and stepped forward to push through the entrance.

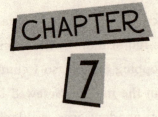

CHAPTER 7

Anything That Can Go Wrong, Will Go Wrong

An old-fashioned bell rang and the door almost hit an old man waiting at the back of a queue that ran for six bodies to the counter. Alongside a Perspex-protected screen was the unprotected newsagent's counter, at which nobody queued. A woman in a sari sat on a stool and watched a tiny television playing loudly.

The line for the post desk stood tightly between a greeting cards stand and a magazine display. Close enough to the old man's cream jacket to smell his Old Spice, my eyes darted around the space, searching for a camera. I couldn't see one, but that didn't mean it didn't exist. Like God. And farts.

Water dripped from my cap's brim. The bright red of

the Arsenal shirt had turned burgundy. With my empty stomach rumbling, I wondered whether I shouldn't give it up and go home for food. I had 8p in my pocket. Maybe the bored-looking woman would pity me and sell a single boiled sweet for a stack of coppers?

The queue moved forward. A man with a huge beard walked through to the door, saying 'Excuse me' over and over as he left. What would happen when the note was read? The question didn't make my chest feel less tight, but it did force my hand to my back pocket.

I hadn't printed my message because I knew they could trace printers. Instead I'd written it left-handed. It had taken a few efforts before I was happy that my block capitals were legible. It would have been embarrassing to be asked to read out particular words and also against the whole point of the note.

The queue moved forward again. I folded the note in half as a woman pushed a toddler through. A rush of air and the doorbell sounded, but nobody joined the queue. Remember: I was doing this for all the right reasons. In a funny way it was actually the right thing to do. My heart beat double fast as I reopened the note. The paper was damp, but the ink hadn't run.

37

PUT ALL YOUR MONEY INTO THIS BAG. DO NOT TAKE BANKNOTES FROM THE BOTTOM OF THE DRAWER. DO NOT SOUND THE ALARM. THE PERSON BEHIND ME IS READY TO SHOOT YOUR ASSISTANT IF I GIVE THE SIGNAL. IF YOU TALK TO THEM, THEY WILL SHOOT YOU.

I refolded the note and shoved it back into my pocket, tight between my backside and my wallet. I'd forgotten my loot bag. Another customer left and the queue moved forward. There were now three people in front and still nobody behind. What could I do for a bag? I looked from the aisle of magazines to the greeting cards. On the bottom shelf was a bag. It was A4 size, pink, and had an image of a *Frozen* princess. It wouldn't hold much money, but it was better than nothing. I leant across to grab it.

'Watch yourself,' said a departing man.

There were now two people until the front desk. I couldn't believe for such a busy post office no one else had entered. The plan was a non-starter if nobody stood behind me. The note would make no sense. Would that be the end of the world?

Think of Beth. Think of all her stuff. Destroyed. By you.

I pulled down my baseball cap even further. The brim

38

squelched wet between thumb and forefinger. If I pulled it any lower, I wouldn't be able to see.

The voices from the TV began to sing. A Bollywood tune – all strings and sitar. It was probably a love song but all it did for me was to excite the bumblebees of anxiety that buzzed against my ribs.

Look, if nobody joined the queue, I'd take it as clear evidence that stealing money was a bad idea. There had been enough clues already.

The next customer left. There was now only one person between me and destiny. As he asked how much it would cost to send a first-class letter to New York, America, I peered round his shoulder at the person behind the Perspex screen. Up until this point, I'd not looked because I didn't want a heart attack.

It was an extremely old woman, possibly the mother or grandmother of the bored sari-wearing TV-watching woman. Her hands shook as she turned over books of stamps. Her hair fell in cotton wisps across a deeply lined forehead. I stopped looking, instead focusing on the void of the old man's back. Even though a grandmother had been my ideal target, now I was faced with one the nerves gripping my heart were joined by a tremendous churning of my stomach – guilt (and hunger).

Because, essentially, I'm a nice guy.

The door opened. I didn't turn at its sound, but remained facing forward. Footsteps sounded across the tight space. A presence. Someone had joined the queue. I daren't turn round. I didn't want to jinx it. Instead I ignored all the strange insect feelings coming from my body, and I pulled out the note.

George Clooney, Al Pacino, Clint Eastwood.

Dylan Thomas.

Maybe I should just go home?

I remembered the rain. I remembered the fire.

I gritted my teeth and jutted my jaw. I was no longer a south-east London loser teenager. I was a Hollywood hero. All I needed to do was hand over a note and the next thing you know I'd be walking out with a Disney bag full of cash. The old woman wouldn't care. She'd seen enough in this world to no longer be surprised by anything. Come on. It wasn't *her* money.

And then . . . a hand on my shoulder. Before I turned I understood what I'd see: the police! Because the game was up. They'd known all along. What had I been thinking?

CHAPTER 8

Be Prepared to Use Your Imagination

'Dylan Thomas! Writing any poetry?'

It wasn't the police. It was worse. It was Miss Riley, my old Year Six teacher. Gulp. Her hair was as mad as the last day at primary. She was grinning full beam and holding a Sainsbury's bag for life. Her perfume, smelling like dying flowers, made me remember spelling tests, circle time and pleas to stop chatting.

'Not yet,' I said, somehow managing not to swear, my voice two octaves higher than usual.

'How's your mother? What year are you in now? You've heard about Beth's house of course? It was in the *News Shopper*. She was ever so good at football, bless her.'

I didn't know which question to answer, so I said, 'Yes'.

equired person behind me, as referenced
but as it was someone I knew, I'd have to
in.

't I?

Ahead of me, the cream-shirted man asked if he might also send a letter to South Africa.

'I shouldn't really be saying this, but they're lucky to get a flat. Housing is prioritised for people in need, I understand, but why there's got to be social housing in London, I don't know, not when house prices are what they are. But you're too young.'

How would I get Miss Riley to stop talking? She had a weird, faraway look in her eyes. I should just walk away. I'd drop the *Frozen* bag and jog on. I couldn't rob the place with her there.

'How can I help, sir?' asked the old woman.

She had a warm, caring voice. Her eyes, I noticed, were the colour of chocolate. She'd called me 'sir'. I don't think I'd ever been called 'sir' before. Silver glasses hung delicately round her neck.

'Umm,' I said, stepping up to place the *Frozen* bag on the counter because my plan in the instant was to pretend to want to buy the bag.

'You didn't need to queue for this, sweetheart. You

could have paid at the till. This is the postal counter.' The old woman had pulled on her glasses and was studying the bag through the glass. 'But that's £2.99, please,' she said.

To make my show of having no money all the more convincing, I went to pull my wallet from my jeans. But, would you know it, the note came with the wallet, gliding softly and terribly to the floor. I bent to retrieve it, but thumped my forehead against the counter and knocked my cap to the floor.

'Aggh,' I said, staggering backwards into a display of birthday cards.

Miss Riley swept forward to grab the note.

'No!' I said, one hand at my head, the other pointing.

'Mind yourself,' said Miss Riley, not giving the note to me, but sliding it through the gap between the screen and counter because, obviously, today wasn't the day for catching any breaks.

'You want to be sending this, do you?' asked the old woman. 'You'll need an envelope.'

Miss Riley laughed. 'Get the boy some paracetamol too! Is your head okay?'

It properly hurt, not just because of my bruised skull, but also because of my growing fear; safe behind the security screen, the old woman was slowly unfolding the paper.

'No,' I said, bending to retrieve my cap. 'Don't read it.'

'Do you need an envelope, Dylan?' asked Miss Riley. 'They won't be expensive.'

Smiling, the old woman read. She looked up from the note. Her smile faded. She frowned. Her mouth opened but no sound emerged.

'I can't make head nor tail of it,' she said. 'Is this your writing? How old are you?'

'Everything okay?' asked Miss Riley. 'I used to be this boy's teacher. Let me help.'

The old woman gestured Miss Riley forward.

A tiny whining sound emerged from my mouth. Was this *actually* happening?

'My eyes,' she said. 'Can you read any of this?'

Miss Riley craned her neck to make sense of the note the old lady held up.

'Well, that first line says to put all your money in the bag. Is this from your mum, Dylan?'

'Are you wanting to make a withdrawal?'

'No,' I said. 'It's a . . .'

I didn't know what it was. Other than an absolute nightmare.

Miss Riley grabbed my arm.

'Dylan,' she said, 'why don't you just read the thing out?'

I shook my head and broke from her grip.

'I just want to buy the *Frozen* bag,' I said, temporarily forgetting that my worldly riches extended to no more than 8p. 'The note's for something else. Not for reading. Thank you.'

Undeterred, the old woman tried reading more. She got so far before beckoning Miss Riley back.

'Do you have a gun?' she asked. 'It says you have a gun. At least, I think that's what it says.'

'No. Just a parcel to send recorded delivery, please.' And then she realised what she'd been asked. 'A what?'

'I've got 8p,' I said, pulling the change from my pocket and piling it up on the counter.

'A gun?' asked Miss Riley.

'It's just a story I'm working on. Can I have it back?'

'Ahh,' said Miss Riley. 'You and your stories. Don't be embarrassed.'

The old woman pointed at the note.

'I've no idea what that last sentence says.'

'When I started teaching, handwriting was an important part of the curriculum,' said Miss Riley.

'Aha!' said the old woman. 'Those two words: *shoot you*. Definitely.'

'I've got to go,' I said. 'I've made a huge mistake.'

I turned and tripped over Miss Riley's shopping, slapping to the floor. Two onions broke for it and rolled under the magazine stand. I pulled myself up, brushed myself down, and pushed through to the front door to safety/freedom.

'You don't want your bag?' called the old woman after me.

'What about your story?' added Miss Riley.

I ignored them both.

On the bus home, I sat on the bottom deck, even though three pit bulls meant the space stank of wet dog. My plan had been to come home with thousands of pounds. In actual fact, the morning had cost me the 8p I'd left in the post office.

But the day hadn't been completely wasted because I'd established that notes and post offices were not the way forward. Even if Miss Riley hadn't magically turned up, I'm not sure I had it in me to take money from the old woman. All thoughts of insurance had flown from my brain when I'd watched her read my note.

Maybe I needed to find a post office, or a bank,

operated by Hitler. Someone so evil they deserved to be robbed.

Maybe banks *were* the way to go, Dad was always on about how they were run by crooks, one rule for them, another for us, that kind of thing. And in the unlikely event that I were caught, I could always play stupid and say I thought Dad was talking literally, which meant I didn't realise I was breaking the law, officer.

Banks.

Fewer threats of violence.

Yeah.

Back home, Dad was snoring on the sofa as gunshots sounded across the front room. I took to my computer and headed straight for Google Maps, pausing only to check Beth's Facebook to see she'd actually posted something for once – a sad-faced emoji, which didn't necessarily have anything to do with me burning down her uninsured home and forcing her family to move into a cramped high-rise flat, but still . . .

CHAPTER 9

'Ever Tried. Ever Failed. No Matter. Try Again.
Fail Again. Fail Better.' Samuel Beckett

'Have you considered offices?' asked Dad from the sofa.
'Better an office than a ladder, I'm telling you. Accidents
happen on ladders.'

Dad flicked through *Sight & Sound* as I thumbed the
BBC Sport app. Palace hadn't bought any players and
the new season was getting closer. Their problem was
the salaries of quality players. How many banks would I
need to rob to be able to buy Palace? Even though they're
crap, they'd still cost hundreds of millions.

Football, bloody hell.

'Did you hear me?' asked Dad. 'Even if you don't get
a summer job in an office, you should think about one

when you're my age. You don't get covered in sewage in offices. Not unless you're really unlucky.'

I glanced up from my iPhone. He'd not shaved in a couple of days. It made him look homeless. I thought of Beth. I looked back to my phone. What now? Notes obviously weren't the way forward. How else do people rob banks? Was there a way of making myself invisible? Like when you're at a popular kid's birthday party? That'd make the whole robbery thing easier.

Tremors of vibration – a call! I stared open-mouthed at the screen. *Beth!* it said, as if by magic. (I can't remember why I'd put an exclamation mark next to her name but it meant every call from her felt dramatic.)

'A girl?' Dad smiled.

I ignored him, and shot up the stairs past an eye-rolling sister into my room.

'Hey,' I said at the exact moment my back bounced down on to the mattress.

A cat replied. And it mewed. At least, that's what I thought I heard. Maybe Beth had accidentally cat-called me, meaning a cat had slinked across her phone without her knowing.

But no.

'Dylan?' she said and I think the sound was sobbing.

'Are you with a cat?'

She laughed. One of those congested laughs people do when they're crying. I don't know why I asked if she were with a cat. Well, I do: I'm an idiot.

'I'm sorry,' she said, sniffing. There was a sigh like ripped paper. The sobbing stopped. Usual service had resumed. 'I was just feeling a little overwhelmed. How are you doing?'

I closed my eyes, imagining I knew how to talk to women.

'Chilling,' I said and immediately regretted it. 'Not chilling. It's been a weird few days.'

'Yep,' she said. 'Tell me about it. Look. I don't want to unload but . . . do you mind if I unload?'

For a brief, brilliant moment, I thought she was about to lay into Harry.

'No problem,' I said. 'Unload away.'

'So Dad, fresh from the no-insurance revelation, has just announced we've got until the end of August to find, like, six weeks' rent as a deposit.'

'That's lame,' I said, disappointed this wasn't about Harry and not entirely sure what she meant.

'That's, like, thousands of pounds and we've literally got nothing. And if we don't pay, we get evicted.'

'I'm sure something'll work out,' I said. 'Your dad knows people.' The grunting sound coming out of my phone indicated Beth wasn't as confident. 'And, anyway, what if *I* got you the money?'

Beth laughed.

'You? How?'

I thought back to the incident in the post office.

'Winning the lottery?'

'That's sweet, Dylan, but are you even old enough to buy a ticket?'

'No, but *they* don't know that and *we* could go on holiday to, like, Hawaii and pay people to do our GCSEs and did you know the capital of Hawaii is Honolulu?'

'Honolulu?' said Beth.

'It's fun to say.'

'Honolulu,' said Beth again.

'Honolulu,' I replied.

There was a bass rumble down the line, a thumping sound.

'It's Mum,' said Beth. 'I've got to go.'

The line disconnected and I lay staring at the ceiling for a while before creeping back downstairs.

Dad had been waiting.

'There's this film I recorded . . .' he said the very second I walked into the room.

I collapsed into the sofa and as I did so a huge smash broke through the house. Had I broken the chair? No. The sound had come from above. I almost expected Mum to crash through the ceiling, but she didn't. The noise was metallic, like a car hitting another car. Rita and Mum were soon standing in the front room's doorway, faces pulled in alarm. Mum held Rita's hand.

Even though it was late afternoon, Rita was in her pyjamas (decorated with cartoon dogs). Mum wore jogging bottoms and a T-shirt. She often claimed to be going off for a run, but other than the 'activewear', there was no evidence that she ever did. Evidence like leaving the house, for instance.

'What was that?' she asked. 'That noise?'

'It sounded like something hit the roof,' said Rita. 'Like maybe a drone.'

My heart froze at the thought of FBI agents streaming from the attic. They'd found the note. I was done for. This was it – the scene of my arrest. I should have liked to wear something smarter than an old Palace training top. And what if I were put into a cell with a load of Brighton fans?

'Probably just the aerial,' said Dad. 'Sounded like the aerial. It's looked like it was going to fall for months. Don't worry. It's the aerial.'

My heart continued to beat. If I had to imagine what an aerial falling off a roof sounded like, it would have been the exact sound I'd just heard. And the FBI agents would have stormed the front room by now. And, anyway, what would the FBI be doing in Orpington?

Rita pointed at the TV.

'The picture's still there,' she said.

'Kay?' said Mum. 'Are you not going to do *anything*?

Dad, rising and sighing, told Rita that we got our TV from a cable.

I nodded. Idiot.

'Oh,' said Rita.

As Dad looked for his trainers and Rita disappeared upstairs, Mum told me to help my father.

'You wouldn't want him falling off,' she said.

Although it was wet outside, it wasn't raining. It meant Dad could go ahead with climbing up on to the roof to investigate *and* I'd have to expend energy helping him.

CHAPTER 10

Use Technology to Your Advantage

Ours is a small terraced house, built for workers at a brewery long since bust. The roof sits steeply, like an upside-down V, and almost fringes the upstairs windows. The aerial *had* toppled, but hadn't fallen to the ground. It lay across the roof slates held by its white cable.

Dad grabbed a wire cutter from his van. The rear doors creaked.

'Stop gawping and help me with the ladder,' he said, untying it from the van's roof rack.

The ladder, when extended, reached half a metre below the aerial.

'Hold it tight,' said Dad. 'Concentrate. You don't want your father's death on your conscience. You'd turn to drink and foul language.'

He climbed the ladder. It trembled as he rose. The rubber grips on the feet held the grey tarmac and I didn't have to try hard to keep it from slipping. Dad reached the top rung and lowered his chest and stomach to the roof. It was a strange image, as if he'd fallen asleep on top of the house. I wanted to take a picture.

Positioned alongside the aerial, he stretched to cut its cable and set it free.

'I'm just going to let it fall, so mind yourself,' he said. 'I don't want you getting squashed. There'd be a terrible mess to clean up.'

He stretched to get at the white cord.

'Oops,' he said.

The ladder strained with metallic groans. Dad swore.

And, very slowly but with unceasing inevitability, he lost his balance.

He managed to fall head first, knocking the aerial to one side and slipping quickly on his belly down the damp tiles. I jumped from the ladder and briefly stood with my arms out underneath the gutter, as he slid down the slate, at the point where he might land.

He screamed swearwords as his arms, head, chest and legs slipped into empty air.

I braced myself to be struck by Dad's heavy body.

He jolted to a stop. The turn-up of his right jean had caught on a nail. His body swung inwards and smacked against my sister's bedroom window. The glass wobbled but didn't break and Dad hung face down from the guttering.

He swore once more.

Rita appeared at her window, screamed and pulled the curtains together.

Standing under my father's reddening face, a gap of about three metres separating his head from mine, I asked if he were okay.

'Does it look like I'm okay? Get your mother!' he hissed. 'Quickly, Dylan!'

But Mum was already outside, standing next to Rita and holding Rita's hand.

'What should we do?' she asked.

Dad dropped a centimetre as his denim ripped.

Spit rained as he replied.

'Move the ladder, for Christ's sake!'

I moved the ladder. Its legs scraped along the ground.

Upside down, he told me to grip its base.

He managed to get his hands on the sides of the ladder. As he did, the denim tore free and he swung one hundred and eighty degrees. The ladder shifted slightly, but heroically I held it from falling. Dad's legs swept past the top of my head and his feet found a rung. They struck the ladder with a metallic clang.

He was safe.

I stepped out of the way as he climbed down. His face was as red as an Arsenal shirt.

'You okay?' asked Mum. 'You were swearing ever so much . . . the neighbours . . .'

He patted my back.

'Good job, son,' he said. 'What a team. Sorry about the swearing.'

'The aerial's still just hanging there,' said Rita.

Dad ignored her.

We went back to the sofa. Dad brought through a beer from the kitchen. A length of denim trailed from his right leg like a snake had its fangs caught in his ankle. He offered me a beer, but I turned it down. It's best your parents don't think you drink.

'Close shave, Dylan,' he said. 'Close shave. Should get these bad boys framed.' (He meant his jeans.) 'Put them on the wall like footballers do their shirts. I could've died out there. Funny how life turns on insignificant details. Like the type of trousers you're wearing. There's a film in that. *The Right Trousers*.'

He pulled open his beer can. Foam rose and he took the can to his mouth quickly, his eyes rolling.

'Let's watch something,' he said, when he'd finished gulping. 'Take our minds off things.'

As he'd just escaped death, I couldn't say no.

Office Space was funny. In a not-laughing-out-loud, grown-up comedy way. The main character, Peter, gets hypnotised to cope with work stress. But the hypnotist dies of a heart attack before breaking Peter's trance. As a consequence of his altered state, Peter doesn't care about anything and goes through his days only doing stuff that makes him happy. (A bit like Rita.) He gets promoted at work. He gets a sexy girlfriend (young Jennifer Aniston). I guess there's a life lesson there, but, anyway, although it's never made entirely clear, the main character and his friends essentially work for a *bank*. And what do you do when you work for a bank? You conspire to rob the bank.

'Are there loads of films about robbing banks?' I dare to ask Dad.

'It's a whole genre,' he says, without turning from the screen. 'The heist. It's human nature to want something without having to work for it. Like you and your GCSEs.'

As the end credits rolled Dad asked if I fancied another

film. The night was yet young. Rita was out drinking. Mum was exercising. We could easily fit another movie in.

I grunted something noncommittal thinking, *Fine as long as it was nothing with Emma Stone.*

As he scrolled through the options, I thought about *Office Space.* Or, more particularly, Peter's plan for stealing money. Even though the film was set in 1999, before Chelsea or Man City won stuff, Peter didn't use a gun or a note. He used computer code, programmed to take tiny amounts from all the financial transactions managed by the company's servers. The money taken at each calculation would be too small to be noticed. However, because of the huge amount of transactions, the amount of 'stolen' cash would soon grow. This was a film and fictional thieves can't get away with breaking the law, so it turns out the code is faulty. Loads of money is taken over a single weekend and the three robbers are screwed, but—

Dad asked if I preferred the Coen brothers or Wes Anderson. But what if a code like the one in *Office Space* actually existed? What if it could be bought online, on the dark Web, for example? Wouldn't that be an easy and effective way of robbing a bank? Isn't everything electronic these days? You wouldn't even need a balaclava or ski mask.

'Do you think it would work?'

'What?'

'A computer code? To rob a bank?'

'Can't see why not. If they can download pictures of naked celebs from the naked celebs' phones, they can install shady code on a cash machine. Probably happens all the time.'

'Hmm,' I said. 'Hmm.'

Because he was right.

Mum appeared. She was wearing sports clothes, but was also completely sweat-free. In her right hand was half a glass of white wine.

'Can I get my boys anything?' she said. 'Are you about to watch something? Shove up, let us join. What a day!'

She forced herself down on to the sofa, a sofa designed for two, a sofa on which I was now squashed between Mum and Dad.

Plan: I'd pretend to need a slash but wouldn't return. In my bedroom, I'd get on the computer and search the dark Web for code to rob banks. Here was a path forward, and it made me feel light-headed like I'd had a glass or two of Mum's wine.

The MGM lion roared.

'Quick question: what are you going to do about the aerial, Kay?'

'It's not going anywhere,' said Dad. 'Chill.'

CHAPTER
11

Do Your Best to Avoid Violence

If you're thinking I would use my personal email address to buy stuff off the dark Web, you underestimate me. I set up another account.

In my bedroom, I clicked through to Gmail, and, sure enough, I had one new message. It included a direct download link for the ATM hack. This expired after a limited amount of time, so I needed to download it soonish. But if I did download it, which I hadn't 100 per cent decided to do, I wouldn't 100 per cent necessarily use it. For one thing, it required access to a cash machine's USB slot. And this would probably demand a better plan than slipping a USB stick into a machine's port when the cashiers weren't looking. I was too tired to decide now anyway; I'd been woken in the dead of the night by

Rita coming home drunk. There'd been loud accusations and slammed doors. Dad had even shouted, which is something he never does. If they were angry about Rita drinking too much, imagine what they'd be like if they caught me robbing a bank?

As I hovered the pointer over the download link, a metallic scratching came from the roof. Instantly I knew what it was. There followed a bang or two, a moment of silence, a huge crash and a scream. The scream came from outside. After the screamer stopped screaming, they repeated 'Oh my God, oh my God' loudly enough to be heard from my bedroom at the back of the house.

'Dylan!' called Rita, forcing her way into my room, stepping on my clothes like they weren't there. I quit my inbox. Now wasn't the time to be downloading ATM hacks. Her face, earlier pale, now corpse-pallid, meant I didn't complain.

'What?' I said, acting like I'd been sitting there innocently staring at the Google homepage, which was not suspicious at all.

'You've got to see this,' she said. 'It's messed up.'

I followed her downstairs and out through the front door. Outside, shoulder-to-shoulder and facing us, stood Mum and Marge, our sixty-something next-door neighbour. Mum covered her mouth with her hands. Marge was still saying 'Oh my god' but quieter now.

Rita hissed 'Look!' and pointed to our right.

The aerial had finally fallen and speared straight through next-door's cat. The animal was pinned to the turf at the front of our house. It was clearly done for.

'Back inside!' said Mum.

'We need to do something,' I said, determined to act the hero and ignore my stomach's heaving.

'You need to do what you're told,' said Mum.

I took a last look before following Rita back into the house. The cat, I remember, had a fun-size Lion Bar in its mouth.

As it was a special occasion Rita allowed me into her bedroom. We stood behind the net curtains and tried to hear what Mum and Marge were saying. The immediate shock of the violence had passed. They now argued as to whose fault it was. Marge was of the opinion that Mum not only had to clean up the murder scene but also owed compensation for Kevin's death.

'Imagine calling a cat Kevin,' said Rita. 'You're asking for tragedy.'

I could have mentioned how Kevin Phillips once played for Crystal Palace and although he'd not set the league alight he was no tragedy, but as I'd been given the honour of admission into her bedroom I didn't want to compromise my position by being annoying.

The room smelt of a sweetness turned rotten and was done out like a pink princess turned anarchist. On her dressing table, a purse peeked out of a handbag. Clothes littered the floor. Thick books lay among them like dead turtles.

Dad's cinematic sense of timing had him arrive home at this very moment. The van rolled into our driveway without stopping, even as its front bonnet almost kissed the now dead cat and guilty aerial.

'The cavalry's arrived,' said Rita.

We watched Dad slowly pull himself from his van. He was wearing his boiler suit, orange like from Guantanamo Bay because he thought it was funny and it also gave customers something to talk about and remember him by.

'Speared. Like Patrick Troughton in *The Omen*,' he announced.

I tried peering down, but the angle of our position blocked sight of Kevin. We could just about see the aerial's bottom pointing skyward. Broken cable trailed over Rita's window.

Dad stepped out of the frame. Mum and Marge both said 'no'. Marge turned away as Mum covered her mouth in horror.

'There we go,' said Dad. 'You can thank me later.'

From downstairs came the sound of the front door opening and closing. Dad's heavy tread moved through the house to the back door.

As I turned from the window, I heard Marge tell Mum we'd be hearing from her solicitors.

'What's Dad going to do with Kevin?' asked Rita.

'Dunno,' I said. 'Leave him for the foxes?' Rita sat on her bed. 'Looking on the bright side of things, our television aerial spearing next-door's cat probably means Mum and Dad will forget about you getting drunk last night.'

'I doubt it,' said Rita. 'And I wasn't drunk.'

Her Samsung appeared in her hands.

'Dylan!' shouted Dad from downstairs. Rita rolled her eyes in something approaching sympathy. 'I need your help. Wear clothes you don't mind ruining.'

'What if I don't reply to him? What if I never reply?'

'The thing about parents,' said Rita, 'is their infinite stamina. He'll never stop shouting. It's what he does. It's how he's scripted.'

'Dylan! Are you there?' shouted Dad.

'Dad's about to make me shovel up the dead cat. Help.'

Rita checked her social media and ignored me. Dad's boots sounded up the staircase. It would feel like this on death row when you hear the guard's key in your cell door. Time passes quickly when there's something nasty approaching. Like your imminent execution. Or your father with a favour to ask.

Dad threw open the door.

'It's polite to knock,' said Rita.

'It's polite not to get so drunk you vomit over your mother.'

He looked me over and frowned.

'Get changed and come outside,' he said. 'There's a dead cat that needs sorting.'

CHAPTER

12

Get Your Hands Dirty

Dad's van stank of Kevin but Dad didn't care because he possesses selective smelling. He can 'turn his nose off at will'. Dad says a lot of stuff like this. But the truth is: the van smelt of Kevin and it was an unforgettable smell, a smell like burnt hair, a smell like raw meat. You could tell something had died. There was majesty, a ripe finality to the smell. If we'd been pulled over by the police because the brake lights weren't working or the back-left wheel looked wonky they'd have radioed headquarters and asked Dad to open up the back for them, suspecting a suburban serial killer for sure.

Even with the window open, I felt like throwing up. Dad tapped his hands against the steering wheel, roughly in time to the radio. The song had the chorus:

'It's the end of the world as we know it. And I feel fine.'

There was a queue of traffic for the tip. Mostly OAPs in polite hatchbacks full of gardening refuse or whatever. Dad explained the plan as we edged through the industrial estate.

'We get out. You find the closest tip dude and you ask where to chuck metal. While you're doing this, distracting him, I'll dump Kevin.'

I'd assumed there was an incinerator at the tip. Dad *had* said we were going to turn Kevin into ashes because Marge wanted the cat's ashes spread over the front lawn, the place of Kevin's demise. Turns out Dad lied.

'We can't just dump a cat,' I said. 'It's cruel.'

And I had that Spider-Sense tingling that someone was about to get me in trouble. It was a feeling I usually had at school, like that time Tim Parker, my partner in Biology, thought it'd be funny to hide a pig's heart in Charlotte Wiseman's bag. It wasn't funny. And as a consequence Charlotte no longer felt comfortable taking Biology.

'It's only cruel if the cat were alive. It's not alive. An aerial did for it.'

'But Marge . . .'

Dad stopped tapping his hands. He fixed me with a Dad stare.

'We don't have any money, Dylan. You know that. I'd love to take the cat to the most expensive crematorium available to animals; I'd like its ashes to be held in a silver cup with purple velvet lining, even though I hated the thing because it was always getting in the house and stealing chocolate. But the truth is we can't afford to do anything but dispose of the cat as best we can. Here, at the local dump. We're doing Marge a favour. You shovelled the thing up, you know how disgusting that was. So we do what we do and if we had any money, we'd do it better, but we don't, so we compromise. Kevin goes to the dump. Kevin doesn't care.'

There was a shadow of sadness to Dad's words. I didn't push it. The van crawled forward, through the height-restriction markers that loomed like a castle gate. Men in reflective jackets swept lost rubbish into huge piles. Dad swung the van into a box marked by grey lines painted on the ground. In front of us were six huge skips, all full to the brim. Each was marked with a sign indicating what form of refuse they accepted. The skip in front of us was buoyant with broken branches

and black bags vomiting grass cuttings. Its sign said
GARDEN REFUSE.

'Garden refuse is as good a description of a dead cat
as any,' whispered Dad, although no one could hear us
inside the van anyway.

He turned off the engine, the radio fell silent, and he
rolled out of the van, the sweet stink of a thousand houses'
rubbish rolling in. It was a relief from the dead cat.

In the back of the van lay the aerial and Mum's sports
bag, never before seen outside the house.

Dad pointed out a worker a couple of skips away.

'Ask him about the metal,' he said. 'Initiate phase one.'

The skip next to ours was full of metal; you could
even see a few aerials sticking out like mad trees.

'I don't want to,' I said.

Dad spoke between clenched teeth.

'The older you get, the more stuff you have to do that
you don't want to. The world is full of people telling you
to do stuff you don't want to. So just do it.'

I looked at Mum's sports bag. Was the cat in there?
There was no way of finding out unless I opened it. At
this very moment, the bag was both full of cat and empty
of cat. Apart from the smell. Which kind of suggested
there *was* a dead cat in the bag.

'Dad, you're being one of those people right now.'

'Yep,' he said.

I went over to the worker, who was in his twenties and muscular and had tattoos. Dad tiptoed off like a silent-movie villain with Mum's sports bag, which I bet he didn't ask permission to use. I told myself that all things pass and before I knew it, I'd be back home to the comfort of planning bank robberies, and I said to the man, in a voice higher than I wanted:

'Excuse me, where do I put the metal?'

He looked up. He pointed at the sign behind me that said METAL and being distracted from tying up his black bin liner meant he must have caught sight of Dad at the moment Dad was about to launch Mum's sports bag, featuring Kevin, into the garden refuse skip.

'Oi!' he called. 'You!'

Dad froze in a bag-throwing pose.

'That's for garden refuse only. Empty your bag.'

But Dad threw the bag. It spun into the rear of the skip. Broken branches whispered their disapproval as it whistled past.

'It's full of leaves,' said Dad. 'Leaves and grass.'

This response silenced the worker.

Dad made a weird whistling noise and, for my sake, pointed at the van with his thumb. Upping the tempo, we jumped in as the worker, abandoning his rubbish bag, stepped forward, waving his hands. Dad swept into reverse and with a chug of diesel we accelerated away, losing the worker in a fog of exhaust fumes.

'What about the aerial?' I asked.

Dad nodded, smiling.

'Yeah,' he said. 'What about the aerial?' My breathing slowed as we passed the height restriction and pulled out into the wider industrial estate. 'Okay, maybe we should have spent a bit more time on the plan,' said Dad. 'Just don't tell your mother. That was close. We can dump the aerial another day. Take her car.'

We headed home. The stink endured, a smelly ghost, even though Kevin had left us. The aerial rattled with every pothole and speed bump. I checked the wing mirror for police cars. Dad said the worst that might happen in the extremely unlikely event anyone bothered checking the bag before the skip's contents were turned to compost was that he'd get a warning letter from the council. That is, of course, if anyone had made a note of the van's registration plates, which they hadn't.

'The only thing,' he said, 'is we'll need to get ashes from somewhere. To give to Marge. Any ideas?'

The remains of Beth's house had been cleared up, so I had no ideas. About anything any more.

'Amazon?' I said.

CHAPTER
13

Robbing a Bank is Like Riding a Horse

The day hadn't finished with me – there was further awkwardness to come. Almost home, Dad was saying how he'd recorded this film called *Chinatown* and he'd consider having surgery to remove his memories to enjoy it over again, if such surgery existed, and I was definitely old enough to watch it, although it was a slow-burner. He stopped to point through the windscreen to a ginger-haired girl walking with two thick orange shopping bags, and shout, 'That's your friend! Emma Stone . . . what's her name?'

Dad was too quick to pull the van over and sound the horn for me to be able to conjure a reasonable enough excuse for not stopping. I should have told the truth. Life lesson there. Because talking on the phone was one thing but sitting in a van full of Dad's chat and the stink of Kevin was a whole new level of awkwardness.

'Wind down your window.'

'Dad, the van stinks of dead cat.'

Dad leant across my lap to wind down the passenger-side window. I smelt faint coffee. And heavy Kevin. Beth, incredibly, hadn't noticed the transit van coughing to a stop behind her. She continued walking, looking more round-shouldered than the last time I'd seen her. Probably the stress of the high-rise.

Dad, still leaning, shouted into the street.

'Hey! Hey!'

Beth stopped. Dad spoke from the corner of his mouth. 'What's her name?'

'Beth,' I said.

'What?'

'Beth,' I repeated, an increment louder.

'Beth!' called Dad and Beth turned.

I offered a weak smile. She approached the van without speaking. At the passenger door, she paused, putting her bags to the ground. They rustled with embarrassment.

'Hey,' I said.

'Hey,' she replied with a voice filtered free of all colour.

She opened the door. If I'd not been wearing my safety belt, I might have fallen out. Instead I unclicked the catch and shuffled to the middle seat. She retrieved her bags and clambered in. The shopping filled the footwell. My shoulders touched Beth's and Dad's and I wished I'd never got out of bed, like, ever.

The thing about people with ginger hair is they often have the most perfect cream-like skin.

'Sorry about the stink,' I said.

'It's not Dylan. We had an accident with a cat.'

'Oh no,' said Beth. 'That's sad.'

'The cat was called Kevin,' I said, as way of explanation but nobody replied and we drove on.

'So how's life?' asked Dad. 'We've not seen you in a while.'

Beth sighed. 'Okay, Mr Thomas, okay.'

(She didn't look okay. That trembling bottom lip, for one thing.)

'You're in the tower block, right?'

'Daaaad,' I said.

'I'm asking if that's where she wants dropping.'

He could have talked about anything but Beth's flat. Why, Dad? What happens to adults? When and why do they lose their sense of embarrassment? And where does it go? It must be something to do with the accumulated effect of years of drinking alcohol. It kills off the part of the brain governing self-awareness.

'What's wrong with living in a tower block, Dylan?' asked Dad. 'You get a good view. Bet you can see London, can't you, Beth?'

'You can,' said Beth. 'The lights of London. Well, Bromley. Everything's not so great to be honest. Did Dylan tell you about the money?'

'Dylan never tells me anything.'

'We've got to the end of August to find, like, six weeks' rent for a deposit. If we can't, we're out.'

Dad turned and his voice dropped as he said, 'I'm sorry, Beth.'

'It's not your fault,' she said, offering a grin as convincing as the Ralph Lauren they sell at Lewisham market. 'It won't be the end of the world. I'll probably have to move in with my aunt.' I remembered Beth talking about her aunt. 'Mad cat woman' was the way she described her. 'And that'd probably mean moving schools to finish off my GCSEs too. I mean, I'd definitely have to move for A levels.'

Now I turned.

'You what?' I said. 'Move school?'

She nodded. 'Yep.'

(She hadn't said *that* last night.)

The sunlight drained from the day. Everything became one of Dad's black-and-white films.

'That sucks.'

'It does,' Beth agreed.

And even though she hadn't actually answered the question about where she wanted dropping, Dad took the road to the high-rise.

'So . . . have you won the lottery yet, Dylan?' asked Beth, because she had to say something to break the poisonous gas of silence that had settled in the cab.

'Not yet,' I said.

'Dylan's been helping his dad.'

'Really?' Here came Beth's first smile. 'What's the occasion?'

Dad grunted. He was smiling too.

'Exceptional times call for exceptional measures. Our aerial fell off the roof and killed next-door's cat. That was the accident.'

'God, that's terrible,' said Beth, stifling a laugh. 'I thought you meant like you'd run it over.'

'Speared like a kebab,' I said but, again, nobody replied.

The van pulled up outside Beth's high-rise and not

79

soon enough. Of course Dad chose a spot where some kids on bikes were hanging.

'Thanks, Mr Thomas,' said Beth as she pulled the shopping from the van. 'See you then, Dylan. We should meet up or something. Sorry about the cat.'

I didn't offer to help. I didn't move my feet to make it easier. I think the thought of Beth moving school had paralysed me. Nobody else at school looked like Emma Stone. Where did her aunt live? Why hadn't I asked? She couldn't move away. It wasn't fair.

'Take a shower!' I said, which was meant to be a funny thing to say in relation to the stink of dead cat but ended up sounding weird.

Dad didn't instantly drive away.

'She seems different,' he said, watching Beth. 'More glum. Still, she's the kind of kid who'll go places.'

Yeah, to another school, I thought.

She moved towards the gang of kids. One jumped off his bike and took a bag from Beth.

'She's getting mugged,' I said quietly, not moving.

But the group were smiling and Beth was nodding. They were helping her carry the shopping. My words hung in the cab like a dead cat.

'Goes to show there's still gentlemen about, eh?' Dad

laughed as he started the engine. 'You were quick to help her, mate.'

I muttered something about equal rights for women, but my words were lost to the van's engine turning over.

'It really is amazing how much she looks like Emma Stone. Genuinely amazing. She could get money for it.'

We drove away. I focused on the high-rise, my head tracking the tower as it stood like a giant beanstalk to all my fifteen-year-old hopes, until I could see it no longer.

When the van pulled up outside home, Dad undid his seat belt and turned towards me.

Real Talk.

'Buster Keaton broke his neck when filming *Sherlock Jr*.' I knew this. Dad had showed the film to us, like, a hundred times. And, on each screening, he'd point out the bit when Keaton jumps off a train on to the arm of a water tank and is overwhelmed by a torrent of water and would say, 'That's where he broke his neck. Did he give up? No. He had a broken neck but he carried on. He persevered. He finished the film. What I'm trying to say, Dylan, is that life is a series of challenges, not a flat race; it's a circuit with jumps. I'm talking about horse racing. Look, getting what you want isn't easy.'

'Beth . . .' I began.

'You're only fifteen. I'm talking generally. Indiana Jones would never have found the Ark if he'd surrendered at the first hurdle. And he had a giant ball rolling after him. Imagine that. You've not got a giant ball rolling after you. Not literally anyway. Perseverance. It's something I've never been good at. Following your plans through. My screenwriting. Once you've committed to something, you've got to see it through. And, you know what, women find perseverance attractive. And men too. You know. Just saying.'

'Okay, Dad,' I said. 'You managed to get rid of the cat all right.'

Dad looked at me and nodded.

'I did,' he said. 'When I'd decided to chuck Kevin in the dump, I carried it through. Literally. I literally carried it through from the van. Don't tell your mother about the bag, by the way.'

He made me promise.

'And one more thing: there's nothing wrong with living in a tower block.'

Climbing the steps to my room, a strange warmth spread across my body. I never thought I'd think this, but: Dad was right. About the tower block *and* perseverance too. I wasn't going to get down about Beth being sad in the van (that smelt of Kevin). Today was only a hurdle. After I'd seen through my plan and robbed the bank and Beth had forgiven me and maybe even more, we'd look back at this summer and laugh. We'd say maybe even the house burning down had been a blessing in disguise.

Beth, don't you worry, you're not leaving school. You're not even moving in with your aunt. How? Your boy Dylan is going to rob a bank.

Smiling, I pushed open my bedroom door and saw the back of Rita. She was at my computer. She turned, unsmiling, and said –

'What's an ATM hack?'

CHAPTER 14

Trust Nobody

I stepped into the bedroom and closed the door.

'Why are you on my computer?'

Rita shoved a hand to my chest and pushed me to the bed. I bounced down on to the mattress and the springs squeaked. I couldn't believe I'd left the computer switched on *again*. And I couldn't believe Rita had gone into my bedroom, although I could.

I thought Kevin's death had brought us closer. I thought we'd reached an understanding. Dad's van-chat seemed very distant now.

'Explain or I'll tell Mum and Dad. What are you planning?'

'It's nothing.'

Rita shouted, 'Mum! Dad!'

I looked at her. I made a decision.

'It's a code you install on a cash machine and it enables you to withdraw money without a card.'

'Whose money?'

'The bank's.'

'Will you get caught?'

'I've not done anything yet.'

'But if you install the thing, will you get caught?'

'Like, nothing's foolproof but the website says the code not only turns off the ATM's camera but also makes sure the withdrawal isn't recorded. It's even meant to delete itself from the USB when installed.'

'Really? I mean, I'm not a geek, so I don't know, but really?'

I nodded.

Rita continued to stare, like if she looked hard enough, she might be able to read my mind, which she wouldn't be able to.

'It's because of that girl, isn't it? The one whose house burnt down.'

'No.'

Rita eyed me.

Who was Rita? I mean, she was my sister and all, but who was she really? Was she the kind of person who

85

would (or could) break the law? I'd experienced a lifetime of her telling Mum about the smallest mistakes I'd made.

'But I'm not actually going to rob a bank. You'd have to install the code first. Like, in the ATM's USB slot.'

'The bank in Chislehurst has two freestanding cash machines in its foyer,' she said.

'You'd want one on the outside. Less security.'

'That might be so, Einstein,' she said, 'but the ones in the bank are full units. You're able to get round the back of them and whatever. The one in the wall's just a screen.'

I hate it when my sister talks sense.

She turned back to the computer. I watched her hand move the mouse.

'There,' she said. My focus turned to the back of her head. 'It's downloading.'

I tripped over clothes to get closer. And she was right: it *was* downloading. She'd not even asked.

'You shouldn't,' I said but I didn't feel it. I felt a birthday-morning excitement.

Rita was smiling. 'What've you got to lose?' she asked. 'And the thing is, I'll tell Mum and Dad all about this if you don't at least give it a try. You can help Beth and all I want is a new MacBook for uni, because I'm not greedy, Dylan.'

I thought of all the stuff I'd already done. The notes. The lies. The intrigue.

I thought of sad-eyed Beth.

'Okay. I'll do it. But I'm going to need your help.'

Rita stood from the computer. The chair toppled backwards.

'Forget it,' she said. 'I've got my A-level results coming out in, like, a week and my whole future ahead of me. You're on your own, buster.'

PART 2

CHAPTER 15

Remain Focused, No Matter What

Mum eyed Dad over her coffee mug. She wore a pink dressing gown that clashed with her face. Dad was in jogging bottoms and T-shirt, ready for the working day's boiler suit. I stared nowhere, still half asleep, and ate own-brand Crunchy Nut Cornflakes. Mum had pulled me out of bed. Supposedly it's unhealthy for teenage boys to spend all morning under the duvet, doing I don't know what. When she'd yanked back my curtains I'd hissed like a vampire.

Rita never ate breakfast at the table.

Question: could I dress up as a workman to enter a bank with a USB stick containing an ATM hack?

(By 'dress up', I mean disguise myself.)

'Hello,' I'd say. 'I may look like a schoolboy and I

realise this moustache isn't very convincing but I've been sent from head office with the instruction to inspect your cash machines. In private. Please.'

The polite manager would ask to see my ID. I'd show a home-printed card with a bank logo I'd downloaded. The manager would nod, tell me she'd need to make a phone call and in time the police would show up and I'd be waist-deep in legal shizzle and Mum would be going mental.

I needed a more sophisticated strategy.

'I told Marge £100 and a gravestone because she could get us in court for a lot more,' said Dad.

Mum turned to me as if I should say something. I chewed like a cow and lowered my eyes to the table. What would happen if I told Mum the truth about her sports bag? About Kevin's end? About the box of ashes Dad bought off Amazon with my phone? *I'd* probably be the one in trouble.

'We can't afford £100,' said Mum.

'We can't afford Marge taking us to court.'

'Oh, for God's sake, Kay. She's ancient. She won't take us to court. I don't want a gravestone out front. It'll look hideous. Like something off Jason King.'

'Stephen King,' said Dad. 'And, anyway, I'll make

sure it's discreet. Just "Kevin" and the cat's dates. Trust me. We don't have to dig up the lawn. And OAPs know more lawyers than we do. They have to. What with the wills. You see it on TV. Litigation is a retiree's favourite pastime.'

'If the cat's not being buried, what's the point?'

'Marge wants a stone as a memorial. I can chisel it myself.'

Black coffee splashed across the wood as Mum stood up from the table, her chair screeching against the floor. She muttered bad words about Dad and Marge as she stomped off.

'Women,' said Dad, but looked embarrassed to be saying it. 'Well, not women. Your mother, I mean.' I nodded, chewing. He took a sip from his tea and looked off into the middle distance. He must have been having an adult thought. It passed. 'Fancy helping your dad with some plumbing today?'

'I'm working on my History coursework,' I said.

Dad nodded, standing from the table to fetch a cloth. He wiped up the spilt coffee.

'Good for you, son,' he said. 'Good for you.'

He flashed a Dad smile but I could see he wasn't thinking about his son.

I changed the subject. I talked about *Chinatown* and how I didn't understand what was going on.

'Well,' said Dad. 'The thing about *Chinatown* is you're not meant to understand it . . . like marriage really.'

Later, Rita was standing in my bedroom and saying 'So what do you want?'

I'd WhatsApped her. For the first time ever. This was the summer for doing original things.

My room.

I'd sent this because, even though WhatsApp has government-standard encryption, Mum, the ultimate authority, could still demand to see my messages. I didn't want there to be anything incriminating, should I forget to delete them. Like that time a stranger sent me a picture of Megan Fox in a bikini.

In the interest of full disclosure, I'd actually sent Beth the message first. Accidentally. Because that's the way your mind works. It's called your subconscious and is to blame when you have weird dreams about riding dogs through railway tunnels and the like.

It was exactly when pressing SEND that I'd realised what I'd done. And so I'd quickly thumbed out a further message, saying:

Butt txt. Soz.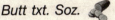

I'd waited five minutes before sending another.

Meet up soon? Come over?

And had regretted sending this message too.

Before all this, I'd been lying on my back and trying to work out if I could afford Palace's final pre-season friendly at Bromley. Tickets cost fifteen pounds, which wasn't loads but was fifteen pounds more than I had and fifteen pounds wouldn't be a huge amount to steal for myself, not if I were, like, compensating Beth with thousands . . .

'Your room stinks by the way. Of boy. Which is really disgusting and so not cool.'

Rita tiptoed across the space, avoiding dead glasses and abandoned pants. She pulled back the curtains I'd closed after returning from breakfast, and opened the window. I put down my phone. I was playing it chill. Like the breeze that gingerly entered the room, unsure if it were welcome.

'Rita, I've been thinking about the bank plan. We don't have a bank plan.'

'*You* don't have a bank plan.' She sighed, probably because of money and the beauty of a MacBook Air and how so much depended on me. 'Look,' she said, 'Don't overthink things. You go to the bank, you go into the foyer and you scout the cash machines. And if they've got a USB slot: great. If not, you enter the next stage of your plan, and you can work that out for yourself at home. And, you know what, the last time I used a cash machine I'm double sure there was a USB thing right next to where you put your card. Look it up, Google Images. It's probably for people without fingers; you know, an accessibility thing.'

She turned to my computer.

'Stop,' I said. 'We can't be searching for stuff like that. They track your websites.'

'Who's they, Dylan?'

'The police?'

She scoffed.

'And Mum and Dad.'

'Dad can't work the toaster, let alone uncover your browser history.'

'What I'm trying to say, sister, is that banks don't just allow anyone to walk in and start fiddling with their cash machines.'

'You'd be scouting the location, Dylan. Like in the films. That's all I'm suggesting. Jesus, I won't bother next time. Thanks very much.'

Rita leant against the windowsill. We didn't say anything. The smell of confrontation filled the room. And it didn't smell nice. I thought back to last night's *Chinatown*. It was boring and confusing.

'Dad says that Marge wants a gravestone for Kevin on the front lawn,' I said.

Rita shook her head.

'Thank *God* I'm leaving home.'

Silence fell. But Rita lingered.

'Look,' I said, feeling like the rest of my life was pinned to this moment, 'if you give me a lift to the bank, I agree it makes sense to at least look at the cash machines.'

'I'll get dressed,' said Rita, already halfway out of my room. 'We wear black, right? And forget about me getting out of the car, that's not happening.'

I grabbed a USB drive from my desk drawer and transferred the code. At 100 per cent, I made sure I ejected the USB before pulling it out (a little too hard because it slipped from my fingers and dropped back into the desk drawer like even it knew the whole plan was a bad idea).

But why should I feel nervous? I'd already threatened a nice old lady in an attempt to rob a post office. All that would happen today was that I'd spend thirty seconds confirming the bank in Chislehurst had no cash machines with USB ports accessible by the public. I might even buy some chips afterwards.

Turns out I was wrong. About what would happen in the Chislehurst bank. *And* about the chips.

CHAPTER 16

Do Your Homework (Scout the Location)

Mum had taken the train to work, so the car was free. True to her word, Rita wore all black. Black tracksuit bottoms, black T-shirt and a black baseball cap I'd never seen before. She looked like she was attending a jogger's funeral.

'Chislehurst?' she said, adjusting the rear-view mirror.

I grunted. During the journey, I got a reply from Beth. It was a winking emoji. I didn't know what to make of it. I wish I were better at interpreting stuff. If I'd had better English teachers, life would be easier.

There was a car park alongside the bank. There was also fuss as Rita asked if I had money for a ticket. I told her I'd brought the USB and nothing else for reasons of security because I thought it was best to keep possessions to a minimum and, anyway, she said she was going to stay in the car, so why did we need a ticket?

The tarmac was pretty much empty, apart from a few Range Rovers belonging to self-made businessmen (this *was* Chislehurst). There'd be no traffic wardens and even if there were, she could drive down the road or talk her way out of a fine because, credit due, she's always been good at charming her way out of stuff, especially with parents.

Rita rolled her eyes.

'Say you actually get your code, or whatever, on to the machine. You don't want traffic wardens remembering conversations with total babes dressed all in black, do you? It's all about precautions. We don't want the Man making links. Think.'

I couldn't work out whether she was bullying me or not. Either way, Mum kept change in an old fabric pencil case in the glove compartment and I paid for half an hour.

'Happy?' I asked Rita, passing her the ticket through the driver's side window.

'Just go and do what you've got to do,' she said like a mother instructing her child to visit the toilet before a long journey. 'If the slot isn't obvious, have a proper look round the back. Make like you're doing up your laces or you dropped your phone.' I turned away, manfully resisting the temptation to ask her to come too because I felt weirdly exposed.

'And Dylan?'

I stopped and turned.

'Play it safe.'

I nodded. I continued my journey to the bank, ignoring, as was the plan, the external cash machine. 'Don't talk to anyone!'

Whatever you might think after reading about the things I've done, I'm not a confident person. Show me a fifteen-year-old who's proper confident and I'll show you an asshat. Apart from girls. They have this freaky all-knowing confidence. Take Beth, for instance. There's something in her eyes that says 'I know'. Looking like Emma Stone must help, but me: I have to battle against the interior voice that claims everyone in the world is judging. Judging the clothes I wear when I go to the corner shop or judging the sound of my voice when I ask for a pint of milk. So I was nervous as I passed through the bank's shimmering glass doors into a room of strangers who would turn and look and think things. Hell is other people looking at you. There was either going to be a USB slot or there wasn't. That was a binary I could deal with. Interactions with strangers were less straightforward.

Inside the bank, there *were* people. But they didn't turn. Because people don't care about you as much as you think they do.

The space was a large square, a single room. Ceiling strips fizzed, and the only natural light came from the doors, doors that faced the wall of cashier desks set behind a stretch of Perspex. In the two far corners, where the wall met the low ceiling, were cameras. Each winked a red light. One cashier served a fat man in a suit. Waiting behind a stretched fabric queue belt was a woman and a silent pushchair. Six comfy chairs were arranged round three low tables at the wall to my left. An old man and an old woman, both with sticks, somebody's grandparents, dressed for church or Wetherspoon's, sat doing nothing, waiting for something, maybe death. Against the right wall were two cash machines. A cardboard sign hung over them, an arrow pointing downwards with the word WITHDRAWALS.

I didn't look at the cameras or anyone else in the room as I made like I was taking my wallet out and swaggered to the closest cash machine as if it were the most natural thing in the world. The screen blinked the bank's logo and a mortgage advert. It was surrounded by silver metal the colour of a kitchen sink. Underneath were the silver numeric keys, the red CANCEL, yellow CLEAR, and green ENTER buttons. There was an opening, a mouth, under the screen where the money emerged. There was another slit up in the top right-hand corner, labelled RECEIPT and underneath this a slot for your card with the label CARD above it. There was also a sticker with a picture of a card and an arrow underneath in case you were an idiot. And below this was a small black square that looked like an IR sensor.

There was also a small wedge that stuck out next to the card slot. And a headphone port and an image of some headphones for people with reduced hearing. Why you need to be able to hear the cash machine, I don't know. They do make a nice rustling sound when they deliver your money, I suppose.

The sister machine was exactly the same. No USB slots. Because – why would there be?

The cash machines stood out from the wall, like two dwarf wardrobes. There wasn't any obvious way into them, no power leads snaking away. I dropped to my knees to look at the bottom portion of the closest one.

It was a smooth grey plastic, a few black marks close to the carpet where people's shoes had scuffed it. The cover felt hotter than you'd expect. It'd have been my luck if the thing had spontaneously gone up in flames as I touched it.

'Can I help?'

Looming over me was a man.

CHAPTER 17

Short-term Pain for Long-term Gain

The man wore a corporate tie and a black rectangular name badge. It announced him to be 'Max Gradual', the branch manager. I took all this in while raising myself from a kneeling position, as if having just been knighted, and I said, *Yes, all was okay and I was going home now, so—*

The automatic doors shivered open, even though there was nobody close. I turned to watch their movement, then realised that this made me look suspicious as if I were contemplating running off, which I was.

'I've been watching you, young man,' said Gradual. 'You seem very interested in our cash machines.'

I felt the force of an audience: the old couple, the woman with the buggy – they'd forgotten why they'd come to the bank. Their reason for being was now me.

'I'm doing a school project,' I said. 'On cash machines.'

Gradual nodded. He smiled like he was about to bite. His teeth were coffee-coloured.

'A project, eh?' he said. 'A project? A project about cash machines? Tell me about your project about cash machines. Maybe we'll be able to help with your project about cash machines. A project! I love projects. And these *are* cash machines.'

The kid in the buggy began crying. His mum fussed to find a dummy. The kid was silenced.

'It's for English,' I said and regretted my subject choice. Of all my GCSEs, English was a poor choice for a cash machine project. Although, I could have chosen French, which would have been worse because I don't know the French for cash machine. *Machine d'argent?* I don't know the French for most things.

'So what were you looking for? How can I help? With your project?'

The manager stared me down with such intensity that I could see the tiny threads of blood appear in the whites of his eyes. And his voice: he'd barked, he'd properly barked. But . . . his words, his questions . . . was he trying to help? Did I dare ask about USB slots? I mean, I'd not done anything wrong. I'd looked at his cash machines.

It was because I was a teenager. In his middle-aged, slightly scary eyes, my age meant I was trouble. And that's prejudice.

'It doesn't matter,' I said as I heard the automatic doors hiss open again and decided I'd take the sound as a prompt to leave.

'What's up?'

My sister's voice. And she was standing next to me. Still looking like an evil athlete in her all-black get-up. But not in the car. *Good job I got a ticket*, I thought.

'I'm Max Gradual, branch manager. Who are you?'

'I'm this kid's sister. What's the problem?'

'Give the boy a break,' said the old woman. The room's focus turned to her. 'He wasn't doing anything wrong, were you, love? Crawling about, that's all. For his project.'

I bit my bottom lip like I was a cute toddler or something. Gradual straightened his back an increment, no longer bending over to pin me down with his stare.

'Did you ask him?' Rita asked me.

She couldn't. Was she? I mean, she knew this was a mistake. It was obvious it was a mistake. All this. What was I ever thinking? You can't be asking about the security of USB ports. It's all about the secrecy.

The woman with the baby spoke. She wasn't queuing

any longer; there was nobody at the cashier's window. The fat businessman had left without me noticing and the cashier, a young woman who might be fit, stared at the action through the glass, resting her possibly fit face in her hand.

'He said he was doing a project. Didn't you?' said the mother.

I nodded. Because that's exactly what I'd said.

Gradual's eyes darted around the space to meet the gaze of the audience: the old couple, the mother, the cashier, Rita. He attempted a smile, which looked more like he was reacting to having his privates placed in a vice.

'He didn't ask for a job? He was meant to ask for a job,' said Rita. 'You were meant to ask for a job.'

Gradual shook his head. I shook my head. My mouth was suddenly dry. I wanted to tell Rita that we should leave. I wanted to tell Rita that I didn't want a job. We could be unemployed together. But I'd need a glass of water to do that.

'We're not hiring,' said the manager. 'And how old are you? I thought you were at school. Doing your project.'

His tone had shifted. He was on the defensive.

'Give the boy a job,' said the old man.

108

'Saturday morning,' said Rita. 'A schoolboy trainee. You're open Saturday mornings, right? The thing is, ever since our parents died, we've struggled for money and not only that but the discipline and organisation required to work in such an obviously well-run bank is just what the boy needs. I said our parents were dead, didn't I?'

Things were unravelling. Like the life status of Mum and Dad. What if I ran outside? The people would forget about us. They'd think it was a joke. I could deal with Rita later. I wasn't yet an adult. I was well within my rights, and expectations of fifteen-year-olds' behaviour, to run away.

But my feet didn't move. I was rooted to the carpet.

'They're open Saturday morning,' said the mother and the cashier nodded behind her. 'You poor children. Give the boy a chance.'

'So sad,' said the old man. 'Go on. A Saturday job.'

Allegiances shifted. Suddenly Gradual was my only ally in the room. We were united in not wanting me to work here. Not least because I was planning to rob the place, not that he knew that. It was all very well for Rita in her Nike Death outfit, but I'd be the first person they'd suspect when the cash went missing: the ace teenager recently hired, having been discovered inspecting the cash machines and claiming he was doing a school project. He'd always been so quiet, so friendly.

'I don't know,' I said, looking down at my dirty Converse.

'I don't know,' said Gradual, looking down at his sensible leather shoes.

'We have the part-time school-age temp scheme,' called the cashier, offering a thumbs-up.

'The poor boy,' said the old man. 'An orphan.'

'Well, I'd need to see your CV,' said Gradual. 'And your parents really are dead?'

'Umm,' I said because my parents, as far as I knew, weren't dead.

'Yes,' said Rita. 'Really dead. Completely dead.'

'My parents have passed away too. An accident up Ben Nevis. Look, what's your name?'

'I'm not sure . . .' I began.

'Dylan,' said Rita.

'Dylan,' said Gradual. 'Maybe we'll be able to find you something. It just so happens our part-time school-age temp recently left us.' There were muted cheers around the bank branch. 'But being in school doesn't mean we don't expect you to work hard. On the contrary.'

'Thank you so much,' said Rita. 'We'll email you his details.'

'My email's on the website. Or drop it round. Whatever's easiest.'

He'd said 'whatever's easiest'. This was a deep change in the man who was bellowing at me three minutes earlier. Gradual didn't seem like a 'whatever's easiest' type of guy.

'Thanks again,' said Rita, grabbing the manager's hand and shaking it wildly. He stood dazed. 'Shake his hand,' she said to me, releasing her grip.

'Well, I'll need to see his CV first. And a covering letter. And the Saturday position is more training than job, so it won't pay much.'

He was speaking for the sake of the audience. He was trying to wrestle control from Rita. It had been simpler for him before she'd turned up. Simpler for me too.

But I did as I was told. I shook his hand. I said thanks. And we left. A wave to the cashier, the mother, the two OAPs.

Inside the car, buckling my safety belt, I asked Rita what had just happened.

'I got you access, that's what,' she said. 'You're our insider.'

'I don't want to work there, Rita. I'm fifteen and I've got GCSEs to do.'

'I don't *want* an ungrateful brother, but some things you've just got to put up with. Did you check the colour of the guy's teeth? Gross.'

She started the engine and reversed the car out of the parking bay. A passing Range Rover sounded its horn but Rita didn't react.

I thought back to what Dad had said about how being an adult was coping with a succession of people telling you to do things you don't want to do.

'How did you know the machines didn't have USB slots?' I asked. 'You came in banging on about our parents being dead and getting me a job, but you never asked about the USB slots.'

'Don't be an idiot all your life.'

All right, I thought, feeling the heat of my blood increase by a degree, *I'll take your job. And you know what else I'll do? I'll rob the bank of tens, maybe hundreds, of thousands of pounds and then we'll see who's the idiot when you're begging me to buy you a MacBook Air.*

And, I reasoned, even if everything went wrong and the bank never got robbed, at least I'd have earned some cash. I could buy Beth one of those tiny mirrors that women have in their purses. That'd be a sensitive gift. It could have a little jewelled whale design. It would show I understood women. Unlike Harry, for instance. And, you know, it might not be thousands of pounds and it might not compensate her for burning down her house or pay for a deposit, but, as Mum says every Christmas, it's the thought that counts.

'Whatever,' I said to Rita. 'What. Ever.'

At least Mum and Dad would be pleased. About me getting a job.

CHAPTER 18

Nothing is Free, Not Even Stolen Money

Mum made Rita give me a lift to the bank. Rita didn't even complain. She was all smiles. Her A-level results had come through and she'd got into Manchester, her first-choice uni. Mum and Dad had bought her a netbook to celebrate, the type you get from Amazon and are 100 per cent plastic, a bit like Rita's smile when she unwrapped the thing.

'Say you text a friend but the friend never texts back even though you know they've received the message. That ever happen to you?' I asked, all innocent.

My elbow was out of the window. Because I was to be inside a bank all morning, it was sunny for once.

'Is it a girl, Dylan?'

'No,' I said.

(It was. The night before I'd messaged Beth about my new job. I'd accidentally added the ghost emoji, which was a slip of the finger. I'd meant to send a sad face.)

'Is it the one whose house burnt down?'

'No,' I lied.

'Don't sweat it,' said Rita. 'Either she loves you and doesn't want to seem keen. Or she hates you and can't be bothered.'

Rita's ice-cold assassin eyes were hidden behind a pair of fake Ray-Bans. She dropped me off in the car park and wished me luck.

'Just make like it's a regular Saturday job. Don't do anything weird. Don't draw attention to yourself.'

There's a bit in *The Godfather* where Al Pacino's character, Michael Corleone, meets with the police commissioner and some other guy (another mafia type?) in a restaurant. They trust Al because he's not yet part of the family. What they don't know is there's a handgun hidden in the toilet. To the sound of subway cars, Michael is frisked, eats some pasta, then excuses himself for a wee, finds the gun and shoots the men. It's all very tense.

Walking into the bank that Saturday morning, I felt a lot like Michael Corleone.

115

One hour later, I was standing in a broom cupboard, watching clouds rise from a tiny plastic kettle, large enough to hold water for only one mug. The paint round the single, naked low-watt bulb had bubbled through the many years of steam created by quick cuppas for the branch manager. At my every movement, the light sent weird, heavy shadows against the walls.

I couldn't imagine Al Pacino ever having to do this.

'Milk, two sugars,' I repeated like a mantra.

I stood in grey trousers and a white shirt, both from school. They'd found a branded tie. Red, with a frayed end, it looked like it was on fire.

The boiling water bubbled with excitement. The kettle switched off. I pulled my phone from my trousers and checked the time. Ten. So many hours before I could go home. Maybe enough time to watch two football matches. And football matches go on for ages. Especially when you're watching Palace. How many more cups of tea would Gradual want? I checked my other pocket. The USB drive was still there. It would be bad to lose it.

A klaxon sounded.

It was instantly jet-engine loud. I jumped, nearly knocking Gradual's WHEN I GROW UP I WANT TO BE A BANK MANAGER mug from the top of the mini fridge.

Not only did the sound, a mix between a scream and a bus reversing, fill the space but it also filled my skull from earhole to earhole. I staggered out of the broom cupboard/employee's refreshment station into the back corridor. What was going on? Was there a fire? I couldn't see any smoke; the air was air-conditioned and tasted like the Underground. The corridor was empty and the alarm continued its insistent pulse, so I tried the first door I found. The door didn't move. Security. I pulled a credit-card-sized piece of plastic from my trousers and touched it, Oyster-style, against the white plastic reader mounted on the wall. An LED above the reader flashed green and the door opened to the cashiers' desks, not where I'd wanted to go – an enclosed space further from the exit. Sitting there with her elbows on her desk was cashier Jaz, introduced by Gradual as 'Jasmine'. He'd described her as having 'efficiency in inverse proportion to the intensity of the previous night's partying'. Now she was looking straight ahead at a pair of customers and not just any pair of customers but Dave, the school bully/ fan of Lion Bars, and his dad. Both stood like crap statues with their hands over their ears and their faces pulled. My first thought was they were robbing the place! No fair! I was here first! But then I realised they were acting

117

weirdly for robbers because they'd probably want to be escaping, what with the alarm.

I stepped over to Jaz.

'Jaz,' I said, but she couldn't hear because of the ongoing klaxon that got right into your brain and made your synapses twitch like fish on a riverbank.

Dave, keeping his hands over his ears, raised his head a degree to acknowledge me.

The alarm stopped at the exact moment I shouted 'Jaz!' Her shoulders jumped at her sudden and loud name. She turned, frowned, and swept her smile back to Dave and his dad, whose hands dropped as Jaz apologised for the alarm. There was nobody else in the bank.

'We get this sometimes,' she said. 'Nothing to worry about.'

But Dave's dad was looking my way and pointing his finger and, for a second, I thought he might inexplicably accuse me of getting his son arrested for ordering a stun gun. Then I remembered that I'd only *imagined* that joyful occasion. His eyes flicked to my name badge.

'Dylan,' he said a little too loudly because his ears were probably still adjusting to the absence of alarm. 'David, isn't that your friend?'

David gave me the look he normally employed when

about to call me a muppet or steal my Lion Bar but, instead of doing either, his face softened like he'd farted and he said 'Yeah. Dylan, how are you, bruv?'

I nodded. 'You know,' I said. 'In a bank. Saturday jobbing.'

'Yeah,' said Dave.

Dave's dad addressed Jaz.

'You've not got any more Saturday positions going, have you? If we'd have known there were vacancies, we'd have had David here first thing.' His voice went weird, low and uncertain. 'Good for you, Dylan.'

'I . . .' said David.

'We're here to sort out David a bank account before he's off to boarding school.'

'Boarding?' I said. 'Like skateboarding?'

'No,' said Dave.

'Not like skateboarding. Like boarding boarding,' said Dave's dad. 'A change of scenery. You heard about what happened with the Lion Bar?' I shook my head. 'He demanded a plain-clothed police officer hand over their chocolate. Didn't you, David?'

'Daaaad,' said Dave. 'I thought they were a kid.'

His dad shook his head, opened his mouth to say something more, but stopped, looking over my shoulder.

I turned to see Gradual standing there with his weasel smile. I'd already noticed his ability to appear in places without warning, like he could teleport himself from room to room silently. (But if he did possess that power, he'd probably be using it for more lucrative/impressive purposes than managing a suburban bank – he'd go and work in Blackheath or Greenwich, for a start.)

'Thomas,' he said.

'Dylan,' I corrected and he offered an embarrassed smile to the watching customers, blinking.

'I know. I've been looking for you. I need your help with something. Jasmine, when you've finished serving these gentlemen, could you give Bromley station a call and let them know it's another pigeon, not that they're bothered. Thanking you.'

He held open the door and I passed through to the corridor. Gradual stepped out and kept his palm on the door to stop it slamming. I waited for the terminal click of the locking mechanism. He smiled as he spoke, revealing those coffee-bean teeth.

'First thing: don't correct your line manager in front of customers. It doesn't create the right impression. Secondly: where's my tea? Thirdly: what are you like with birds?'

CHAPTER 19

A Good Thief is a Good Actor

Being a cubicle in the corner of a room, the toilet was unisex and so created anxiety as I imagined walking in on Jaz. Weirdly the space was much bigger than the broom cupboard/staff refreshment station. In the corner, blocked off by two slabs of plastic, like budget coffin lids, was the toilet itself. Aside from the sink, a wastepaper bin, a hand-dryer, and a stained mirror, the rest of the room was dead space.

I stood at the door, looking across the emptiness, my hands behind my back. There was a smell to the room, the smell of bird. An ill, acidic bird who had pooped everywhere. And I had my eyes fixed on the origin of the mess – a pigeon. The pigeon was looking back, a bit like how Dave had looked at me, with tiny pink eyes. It was standing on the white enamel of the sink, alongside a plastic bottle of lavender-scented soap. There was a small, barred window on the same wall as the sink. Despite a laminated sign underneath that said, in Comic Sans, UNDER NO CIRCUMSTANCES OPEN THIS WINDOW, the window *had* been opened. Gradual had said local pigeons liked squeezing through it and, somehow, triggering the bank's alarm. And it turns out that dealing with these pigeons is the responsibility of the Saturday-morning kid.

The pigeon cooed. And it was a soothing sound, as if to say, 'Hey, bro. At least I did my business in the bathroom.' Of the two other bank employees I'd been introduced to who weren't Max Gradual, the window-opener was obviously Tom. Tom was all arms and legs; you'd think he was a basketball player if you passed him in the street. And he had been grinning wildly, like a madman or a 'before' dentist's ad, when Gradual had introduced us.

'Tell him,' Gradual had said. 'Get it out of the way.'

Grinning, Tom explained:

'When I was six, I got kicked in the head by a llama. I was fine but I've never stopped grinning. The llama damaged a part of my brain. The part that controls grinning.'

'Wow,' I'd said. 'Like the Joker.'

'The Joker never got kicked by a llama,' Jaz had said.

'You're fine, aren't you, Tom? It's only a problem when customers are turned down for a mortgage or are making a complaint.'

'They don't like you grinning when they're making a complaint.'

Using a selection of swearwords, Tom went on to explain how much customers didn't like you grinning when they're making complaints. Gradual had then told Tom to watch his language and he'd told him enough times and another problem with his brain was his memory.

I had no plan for the pigeon. And it wasn't so much that being asked to catch the bird wasn't fair, it was that spending time grabbing pigeons in the toilet (euphemism klaxon), was time not spent identifying whether the cash machines had USB slots. And, actually, having to catch a bird wasn't fair because I didn't even have any gloves. I imagined the feathers were as greasy as Dad's hair after a weekend of sofa-lying.

The door opened, pushing me forward.

'Sorry,' said Tom from the corridor.

He was grinning alongside a flatbed trolley with a cardboard box too small for a flatbed trolley, because why not carry it? I was quickly learning that work (and, by extension, adults) made no sense.

'It's fine,' I said. 'I wasn't doing anything like –' I didn't know which words to use – 'having a poo.'

Tom stooped to look past me.

'Unlike the pigeon!' he said. 'I heard the alarm.' He was smiling. It was the same smile he'd had on his face all morning. 'Want to know how to trap the bastard? Hold the door open for me and don't tell Max.' I held the door as he manoeuvred the trolley into the bathroom. Inside, he told me to lock the door. I hesitated. I'd only ever been locked in a toilet with my dad. Truly, having a job was opening a whole new world of experiences. 'Help me with this.'

A Stanley knife appeared in his hand. Before I had reason to get worried about the sudden blade and the innocent pigeon, he was cutting through the brown tape that kept the cardboard box shut. Opening the flaps, he pulled out three packages, two black and one grey. In total, they weren't that big – you could fit all three into the box my Converse had come in. But, as they caught the light, I could see what they contained.

Banknotes.

Tom lifted the empty box, about the size of a Frisbee, and held it in front of him, telling me to watch and learn. He walked purposefully towards the pigeon, telescopic legs carrying him forward. At the sink, he dived to close the box over the bird.

Success! There was a ruffle of feathers, like pages of a book being turned. Tom lifted the box containing the pigeon, and slid its open side against the wall. His technique was similar to how you might catch a spider with a glass. Only it was a pigeon and he used a cardboard box.

The box trembled and Tom swore, but he was successful in dragging the cardboard up to the window. With a shake, a wild cooing and a squib of feathers, the pigeon was gone – off through the bars and into the dirty sunshine of south-east London.

'Sorted,' said Tom. 'And that's how you deal with a pigeon. Now you can give me a hand filling the last cash machine.'

The bathroom was a gasp of brown feathers and white smears, as if the bird had been protesting about getting turned down for a mortgage for a really nice nest. But I didn't care – here was the moment not only the whole morning had been leading to but the whole summer and maybe even my whole life.

GIVE ME A HAND FILLING THE LAST CASH MACHINE, the man had said.

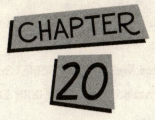

CHAPTER 20

Take Care of the Present and the Future Will Look After Itself

I'd not even had to ask. In fact, I'd played the whole morning pretty chill, without talking about the cash machines even once. This was partly because I was frightened of Max Gradual but also because I was deep undercover like Keanu Reeves in *Point Break*.

'I'm only filling two of the four cartridges this morning,' Tom said. 'Which means you've just got £30,000 on the trolley here.'

I blew air from my mouth. I couldn't help it. Those sweet wedges of cash covered by plastic. The paper inside had the power to make a lot of people a lot of happy. Like Beth. Or Rita. Or me.

'So how much does the machine hold when full?' (My voice wavered.)

'Four cartridges. Well, that's double what we're loading this morning. What's double £30,000, Dylan?'

'£60,000,' I said.

Wow.

Because £60,000 would cover Beth's deposit. And rent. *And* leave change. For a holiday somewhere hot with, say, a best friend like me and first class all the way.

£60,000.

I needed a wee. The tight bladder of excitement.

'£60,000,' I said.

'Yes, sir,' said Tom. 'That's why you read about people getting at ATMs with JCBs. It's a good figure. Like Pamela Anderson.' He stared at me, grinning. I didn't know who Pamela Anderson was and the reference sounded like a *Top Gear* joke. But I smiled because Tom was going to show me the insides of a cash machine. 'Are you going to help me fill her up, then, so to speak? It's pretty straightforward. You ever filled a photocopier with paper?' I hadn't. 'No problem. You just split open the packages and hand me the cash when I ask for it. Won't take long.'

'That's £30,000?' I asked.

'Yeah. Doesn't look much, does it? You could get it in your rucksack, no problem.'

Hands on the trolley, he stopped.

'You're not planning on robbing the bank, are you?'

It's really difficult to get an angle on someone who's always smiling.

I cleared my throat.

'Umm,' I said.

'Of course you're not.' His voice dropped. 'Because I'm telling you, if anyone's going to rob this place, it's me!'

And he grinned. And he told me to unlock the bathroom door.

The cash machine we filled was the external one, accessed through a panel in the wall at the far end of the corridor. You'd miss it if you didn't know it was there – it was more like the kind of door you'd find under the sink. It needed a keycode and a small key taken from the fob hanging on the belt loop of smart black trousers that stopped miles above Tom's ankles.

'Boobs,' he said as he entered the keycode. 'The last manager was a proper lad. Loved his banter.'

As he knelt at the machine, with his head pretty much the same level as mine because I've already said he was a giant, right, it looked like he was about to take laundry out of the washer. He wasn't, though. I wouldn't have been staring and sweating if he were. He pulled out a drawer from the ATM and let it hang like a dog's tongue in hot weather.

'We'll start with the twenties. Those are in the two black packages. The grey is tens. You'd think they'd make the packaging, like, massively different as opposed to dark grey and black but it just goes to show that nobody knows what they're doing.' He spoke as if he'd said this many times before. He looked straight ahead, into the guts of the ATM. He held out a palm, as large as a dinner plate, ready for cash. As much as the idea of handling £10,000 was crazy exciting, I said, 'Can I have a look?'

Tom said, 'No sweat,' and scooted across the carpet. The insides of the ATM didn't look anything like a computer. I'd expected maybe a sleek black PC lying underneath the actual machinery, but it wasn't anything like that. Just different sections of black plastic and wires and screws. My eyes traced wildly across the components and I decided there was no USB. My stomach chilli-knotted in the disappointment because the thought of £60,000 had over-stimulated my imagination and now, minutes later, being rich was as Venus-distant as it had ever been. But then Tom spoke, waving a sausage-sized finger.

'It's just a computer with moving bits of plastic. Like your PC can eject its drawer, if it still has one, this ejects money.'

'Are the ones in the lobby the same?'

'Pretty much. Only difference is you load them from the front.'

I should have shut my mouth at this point but I didn't and this is what I said:

'What, so it's got USB slots and everything?'

And Tom's finger pointed to a silver flash of metal that was partially hidden by a trailing set of wires.

'There. It's what the engineer uses when he needs to update the operating system. Like when you download a new OS for your phone.'

'That's sick,' I said. Tom nodded. It *was* sick. 'How often does that happen?'

'Like twice a year.'

And the USB drive burnt divine glory in my trouser pocket just like the magic stones in Indiana Jones's bag at the end of *Temple of Doom*, if you've ever seen that. The instructions claimed all I need do was insert the USB stick into the slot and leave it for a minimum of fifteen seconds for the code to download. It could be left there forever, but it needed at least fifteen seconds to ensure the code automatically transferred.

I had the stick, I had access to the ATM's USB slot. The only problem was that an ever-grinning basketball-tall man called Tom, who was filling the machine, blocked my path. I needed to think of a distraction and I needed to think of one fast.

'Let's get started, then,' he said. 'Twenties first.'

I struggled to open the package, just like I can never split Haribo Sour bags. Tom ended up getting his Stanley knife out. He wouldn't let me use it because 'You should never trust a stranger with your knife.' He opened the thing in a second and was quick to dismiss my suggestion that I was okay to load the machine myself.

'Because if you've got other things to do, I can manage, Tom. It's just like a photocopier. You said.'

His two hands closed like pincers round two blocks of twenty-pound notes.

'What, so you can steal twenty pounds? Forget about it. Just keep the cash coming, buddy.'

He turned and his arms disappeared into the cash machine.

I honestly hadn't meant to drop the money. Maybe it

was my subconscious working at a higher level than my conscious mind. It wouldn't take much, to be honest. I had a half-opened package of twenty-pound notes tight to my chest, like the scene in *Alien* when the alien emerges from some dude's ribcage, only it was loads of money emerging from mine. I gripped each side of the kind of collar Tom had made when splitting the plastic, but the wrapping remained hipster-jeans tight across the money. I thought to dig the end of the parcel into my chest and rip back the flaps like you might do with a crazily difficult banana. I had underestimated my strength, though, or at least the weakness of the plastic. With one yank, the parcel split completely, sending thousands of pounds blossoming into the air like confetti at a giant's wedding. For a beautiful moment, the air around us was mad with twenty-pound notes, gently fluttering to the floor, making the same noise as the pigeon's wings earlier. It was an advert for the lottery, the winner throwing his sweet jackpot into the air. Tom pulled back from the cash machine. There was a single twenty-pound note stuck on his forehead. He peeled it off, looking to me with a wide grin.

'Oops,' I said.

'I'm not smiling,' he said, pulling his gaze to inspect the trolley and surrounding floor. Both were carpeted in banknotes. 'I'm *so* not smiling. Max will go mental.' He swept around, slipping slightly on the money, and placed a hand on my back. For a second I thought he might get violent. Instead he pushed me to the cash machine, swapping positions. 'I've got hands like frying pans,' he said. 'You grab the strays over there.'

Like he was lifting dead leaves with wooden boards, he scooped up over £1,000 and dumped the riches on the trolley. He continued grinning and, here, I saw my opportunity. I fell to my knees and picked up a fistful of notes from beneath the ATM. I dumped them on the trolley and saw that Tom wasn't watching; he was concentrating, grin brighter than ever, on his own cash pool. I faced the ATM and already the USB drive was in my hand and already the device was heading inexorably towards the USB port like a shuttle about to dock at a space-station airlock and—

CHAPTER 21

Remember: Everybody Makes Mistakes

'Thomas!'

It was Gradual, his voice trembling along the corridor like an earthquake.

The USB drive was back in my trousers faster than it takes to close a browser window. I swivelled on my knees, sure to have two hands full of money, and I smiled the smile of a cute Year Five. Gradual pumped down the corridor, elbows swinging. His face was purple and his expression the exact opposite of Tom's, who continued to sweep stray notes on to the trolley. I swear his corporate tie was glowing red. Here was the moment for Tom to show he was one of the good guys, to stand up for the underdog (me) against the oppression of the Man.

'Dylan dropped half a cartridge, boss,' he said and grinned.

Gradual stopped at an orphaned twenty. He pointed at it. I crawled to his toecap and picked it up. I handed it to Tom.

'Thanks, bro,' he said.

'Right,' said Gradual, now pointing at me. 'You stand up. You, Tom, you need to ensure all this is loaded into the machine, like, half an hour ago. If there's 50p missing, it's coming off your wages.'

How 50p would be missing when there was nothing smaller than ten pounds, I didn't know. Gradual led me down the corridor, explaining that he'd never seen anything like it on a first day and I had to understand that Gradual was the boss and I should take orders only from him because Tom, in particular, had been kicked in the head by a llama. Stopping at the bathroom door, he knocked and sighed.

'Everybody makes mistakes,' he said. 'It's how you respond to them that's the important thing. But I understand what you've gone through, growing up, so . . . you know.'

My mistake, I thought, *was getting this job*.

There was no response from the bathroom, so with

his feet planted in the hallway, Gradual extended an arm to open the door. The smell of pigeon's insides emerged first. It stung my eyes, having increased in potency since Tom had shaken the bird from the window. In Year Seven, we'd visited the Imperial War Museum and there was a gallery where they'd mocked up a First World War trench. The tour guide was very proud that they'd even got the stink right – and the bathroom smelt exactly like that fake trench. Really disgusting.

'Jesus,' said Gradual, stepping in.

I followed him. To my relief, there was no pigeon, but the room, if anything, was more gross than I remembered. There were only a few parts of the floor that had escaped contact with droppings or dropped feathers or both.

Gradual swept his arms around the space, mouth gaping like he wanted to swear but knew he couldn't because he was management.

'I got rid of the pigeon,' I said, my eyes watering.

'Come with me,' he said.

We stepped out of the room, back into the corridor. Tom remained on his knees at the far end. The pile of notes on the trolley looked like the beginnings of a campfire.

'It's your first day,' said Gradual, 'so I'm going to cut

137

you some slack. But next time I ask you to deal with a pigeon, okay, that not only means getting rid of the pigeon but also everything the pigeon leaves behind.' His tone changed; he attempted warmth. 'Imagine if Jasmine had walked in there. She'd have had a heart attack. It smells like bird hell. And don't think I haven't realised you still haven't made that cup of tea.'

I would have told him that I didn't think getting me to sort out a pigeon infestation was really a fair ask and that I had been making the tea but the alarm had gone off, but he was positioned like a teacher giving you a telling-off and there was no contradicting his authority, even if he was way out of order. So I looked at my contrite school shoes, splattered slightly by pigeon, and I murmured an apology.

'Wait here,' he said. 'I'll get you a bucket and water.'

Gradual marched off and I nodded to Tom who was offering me a thumbs-up and grinning.

Look, I told myself in an attempt to raise my spirits, *you've only been here a few hours and although you hadn't expected to do totally demeaning and disgusting things like catch and clean up after wild pigeons, you were centimetres away from installing the hack code. Centimetres. If opportunity presents itself again, you'll be sure to do it successfully next*

time. And if that's not today, because you've got all the cleaning to do, there's always next Saturday.

That is, spoke the dark, pessimistic side of my interior voice, *if you're ever allowed anywhere near the ATMs again.*

CHAPTER 22

Breaking the Law Isn't Fun

And somehow it came to pass that there was a single week before school started. I had that terrible turning of my insides that I felt every time term was close, like a reduced version of Spider-Man's Spider-Sense but one less helpful when fighting crime. I'd not spent any more time on my History coursework, so I was no closer to finishing my explanation of why America invaded Vietnam. I did still have 1,500 of the 2,000 words *and* a three-slide PowerPoint presentation with images of random soldiers and Americans and helicopters, which I'd knocked out in a week of June afternoon History lessons, though. It shouldn't take too long to finish off. I just needed to find the time.

And we were meant to have read a novel, any novel,

for English and, hello, that wasn't going to happen any time soon. I was more likely to write one.

I *could* rob the bank when back at school. Being in Year Eleven might provide a convincing cover story because who'd commit crimes in their last year of GCSEs? But Beth's deadline for raising a deposit coincided with the end of the holiday. All would be for nothing if I hadn't managed to rob the bank before Beth was forced to move in with her hated aunt. She needed the money and she needed it now. The thought made me want to curl up under my duvet.

But no. *Eyes on the prize, Dylan.* I'd started the summer by burning down her home, I'd finish it by making everything right, by showing how much I'd grown since the destruction of the White House. No more Nepalese scented candles – that was Year Ten Dylan. Year Eleven Dylan robbed banks. Check him. This is what he's capable of. He deserves respect, yo.

I jumped on to my bike next to the newly installed half-circle marker where next-door's cat had been speared.

(Dad had crudely chiselled KEVIN, 200?–2016 into the stone.)

And off I cycled, thinking as I pedalled:

Today, the second Saturday of my employment at the bank,

141

should really, probably *be the day to install the hack code on the cash machine and no excuses. I don't have the patience to go deep undercover and I'd get too bored to be a genuine sleeper cell.*

Realistically, what with the spilt banknotes, the job wasn't a long-term prospect. Don't get me wrong, that was good because if working in the bank had taught me anything, it was that I didn't want to work in a bank. It also taught me that I didn't want to be distracted from studying hard in Year Eleven and getting grades good enough to do A levels. This is what I'd say to Mum and Dad when I got sacked/left by mutual agreement because it would prove I'd been planning for my future, something we're told is important.

Jaz, looking like a vampire who'd not drunk blood for a while, and Tom, grinning, were waiting outside. A grey metal security gate, the sort you see over the entrances to takeaways, covered the doorway. Jaz was on her phone and said 'Hey' as I joined them. Tom was hopping from foot to foot like he'd been hypnotised into believing he was a frog, but it turned out that he just needed a wee.

'Oh my days, just go and do it in the bushes,' said Jaz.

Bouncing from one long leg to the other, Tom said he wouldn't because of the Canada goose. Once a friend had taken a slash in the bushes near a Canada goose and the bird had gone for his johnson.

'Tom!' said Jaz, looking up from her phone and catching my eye and shaking her head. 'There's a kid here.'

'Sorry,' said Tom. 'But it's true. And I'm bursting, buddy.'

I acted like it was fine.

Jaz, thumbs working in a blur, growled at her phone. 'Autocorrect!' she said. 'No, Siri, I don't mean I'm *hugging*, I'm *hanging*.'

'Out last night?' asked Tom, grinning and bouncing like an overexcited chimp.

'Duh,' said Jaz. 'Like yeah. Do you like EDM, Dylan?'

'Yeah,' I said. 'They're great.'

'It's a type of music,' she said.

'Electronic dance music,' said Tom.

'I love EDM,' said Jaz. 'Dancing. Losing yourself in the moment, you know?'

And she raised both hands above her head and gyrated. I felt weird and didn't know where to look and it went on for longer than you'd imagine.

We heard Gradual before we saw him. His motorbike farted aggressively as he rode up. The engine continued to bark as he pulled off his crash helmet, designed to

143

look like Iron Man's head, and chucked it to Tom. He caught it, shouting, 'I really need the toilet,' but Gradual was off, swinging his bike to its parking place at the bins behind the bank.

Soon, wearing biking leathers that reminded me of Dad's Guantanamo boiler suit but black, he made us stand a distance off as he unlocked the front grill. Turning a key in a small box I'd not seen, the protection rose like a portcullis, folding over itself like a window blind. Next there were the three locks on the front door, which, because its automation had yet to be turned on, Gradual had to ask Tom to lend a hand to slide across. I stepped forward but Jaz told me they weren't ready. Gradual had twenty seconds to enter on his own and disarm the alarm system before we could follow. We waited at the open doors. Gradual disappeared off behind the cashiers' desks, with Tom whining like a toddler as he gripped his groin with his huge hands.

When Gradual reappeared in the foyer and gave us the all clear Tom sprinted off to the toilet.

We waited, alongside the foyer ATMs, whose screens blinked with life, as Gradual removed his biking leathers like the worst strip show ever. Jaz said her head was hospital bad as Tom appeared at the door to the cashiers'

desks and, with a red face and very obvious veins on his forehead, said, 'The toilet's still locked!'

'Wait a second,' said Gradual as he pulled at his trousers.

'Honestly, Max, I'm going to wet myself.'

'You should have thought of that before you left home.'

Gradual was taking his time to get out of his leathers. And even when he was free and standing in his white short-sleeved shirt, red tie and smart trousers, he folded his kit up with as much care as an assistant in one of those expensive Bluewater clothes shops.

'They lock the toilet?' I asked Jaz as the two men disappeared.

'They lock everything,' she replied. 'It's a bank, babe.'

I nodded. 'So what do we do now?'

'We wait. Team briefing. You must have missed last Saturday's. So lucky.' She rolled her eyes at her phone. 'You won't believe the Snapchats I get sent. Do you have any painkillers?'

If Max Gradual were the manager of Crystal Palace, even if he were, like, spot on with his tactics and the American owners had given him £1,000,000,000 to spend, we wouldn't win any matches across the season and we'd get relegated from the Premier League by

145

Christmas. Such was the anti-power of his team talk. He made Jaz put away her phone and he checked Tom's bladder and bowels were fully evacuated and he asked if I were ready, calling me 'Thomas' again. Only then did he get started with the morning's briefing. I remember that it began 'And I think it was Shakespeare who said . . .' but, honestly, I can't remember another word after that. It went on for ages and it made Friday-afternoon double Physics seem like the most stimulating thing imaginable. If any of us had any inclination to do our best for God and the stockholders this morning, to go the extra mile, then Gradual's speech would have turned to ashes our enthusiasm to do anything but go home.

It was only when he stopped talking that we realised the speech was over.

'Thomas,' he said, as Tom and Jaz drifted away, 'I've something you might enjoy today. And, don't worry, it's not cleaning up after birds. You like computers, right?'

CHAPTER
23

Avoid Mixing Business with Pleasure

I was set up at an empty cashier's desk with the blind drawn so I wouldn't be distracted by looking at customers and customers didn't think I was a cashier because we wouldn't want that, said Gradual. To my right was the door leading to the stockroom and the safe, but I didn't even care because I had a plan and I had to stick to it. Breaking open safes was as dated as Nokia. And, like in school plays, improvisation would only lead to punishment and failure.

Focus, Dylan.

I'd been given the bank's netbook and a plastic wallet fat with cheques. My instruction, without any explanation of why I was doing it, was to enter into Excel the dates and amounts of all the cheques. I didn't even think cheques existed any more, but there *are* a load of old people in Chislehurst. I mean, it's got a Caffè Nero *and* a Costa.

I must have entered the details of 200 cheques, which hadn't made a dent in the pile, and some of which had dates from years ago, when Jaz swung her chair to face me and said, 'Raise your blind, Dylan.'

For a brief moment of wild panic, I thought she was asking me to serve customers. I didn't want to do that because of Gradual's likely reaction but also because it would mean talking to strangers, which is something I've been instructed to avoid doing since I was a toddler. It's also something I hate. But Jaz smiled and winked and it was the wink that did it.

So I pulled the white cord and the blind drooped deskwards. I pulled the other way and it rose like a reverse guillotine. What it revealed cut me off from all thoughts of counting cheques and also, I admit, robbing banks. And weirdly the sight also sent blood coursing through my frame, some of it ending up at my cheeks. My face flushed like I was eight or something.

Beth.

She stood in an oversized red-and-black checked shirt holding two Styrofoam cups of coffee.

'Hey, D,' she said. 'I never said thanks for the lift home.'

She was smiling and it confused me, but the more I learnt about girls, the more I understood that to be confused *was* to understand.

She was wearing the dolphin necklace. I noticed that all right.

And behind her left shoulder was Harry. He'd had a haircut. Imagine a line drawn round his head at the same level as his eyes. Below it, his hair had been shaved off. Above: loads of the stuff. It looked like his hairdresser had collapsed with a heart attack halfway through the session.

'I—' I said.

Jaz leant across from her empty window and put a hand on my hand.

'He says thanks,' she explained to Beth. 'Go fetch it.'

And she nodded to the door at the end of the cashiers' desks.

There wasn't much room between Jaz's chair and the wall, so there was an embarrassed moment of squeezing. I could hear Harry laughing his Scooby-Doo laugh as I apologised past Jaz's back. But soon I was free and out into the sweet air-conditioned lobby, empty but for Beth. And Harry.

149

I took the coffee and thanked her.

'It's an Americano. I thought it's the sort of coffee you'd drink.'

She handed it over and even through the corrugated cardboard holder, I could feel its heat. I made like I couldn't, though, naturally. Steam rose from the tiny plastic mouth. What had she meant?

'Because it's pretentious,' said Harry. 'And lame.'

'They drink it in films,' said Beth.

'You're pretentious,' I said to Harry. 'Sick haircut, by the way.' I turned to Beth, who was no longer smiling. 'Why do you hang out with him?' I said. 'Even my mum calls him an idiot.'

'Your mum's an idiot,' said Harry.

'Not cool,' said Beth. 'Drink your coffee, Harry.'

'It's too hot.'

'It's a cappuccino,' said Beth, rolling her eyes and I laughed like I understood.

'So I got a job,' I said, suddenly conscious of Jaz's attention.

Beth nodded. 'You've already told me. That's how I knew you were here.'

There was a pause where I think Beth expected me to speak. I wanted to apologise for the ghost emoji but my tongue died. Instead I managed, 'Thanks for the coffee.'

'You're welcome.'

'I'll give you the money. Safe.'

She shook her head as my free hand pretended to look for cash in my pockets.

'Just return the favour some time.'

I will, I thought. *And then some.*

'I will,' I said.

'I like your tie,' said Harry. 'Not.'

I frowned. Adding 'not' at the end of the sentence was Dad irony. Beth turned to Harry, her features softening.

'Harry's not feeling himself,' she said. 'His dog died.'

'Sorry,' I said, making sure I gave him a 1,000-watt smile as Beth's head was still turned. 'The neighbour's cat was killed by our aerial the other day.'

'That's lame,' said Harry. 'Cats are meant to have like . . . catlike reflexes.'

'I'll tell you what's lame. Saying everything is lame.'

And although Beth didn't laugh, you could tell by the warmth of her eyes that she found it funny.

'It's true,' she said to Harry. 'About the cat. Dylan's dad said.'

'His dad says lots of things. Let's go,' said Harry,

turning. 'This place is a buzzkill. It's bare corporate.'

Beth held out a hand like she was going to touch me and I looked at it and she let it fall. I said, 'So,' and she smiled. She said they'd better be going but she'd wanted to surprise me with a coffee because I'd seemed down recently.

'I'm okay. Are you okay?'

'Yeah. I guess. We're moving out of the flat,' she said like it was nothing. 'The deadline's next week.'

'I . . .' I said.

I wanted to tell her all she needed to do was wait because this time next week she'd definitely maybe have tens of thousands of pounds. But I didn't say anything because my face was frozen with this weak-ass grin. And bank robbers need to be discreet.

'My aunt. She's not a huge fan of boys. She prefers cats. I think she's a member of a cult or something. Praise the tabby. So, you know, our days of chilling in the rec are probably over and I'll have to get the train to school until the end of Year Eleven. And then move to this college closer to my aunt. They've offered Mum and Dad a place in Kent somewhere. I don't know. Maybe I'll move to a school down there. But you don't want to hear all this.'

'I'm sorry,' I said.

'It's not your fault.'

She sounded like she had more to say but I spoke over her.

'But you're not changing school. And you're not moving in with your aunt.'

'What? What do you mean?'

'You'll get the money. I've got a feeling.'

'I've got a feeling too . . .' began Harry and was for sure about to call me lame until he'd remembered how I'd rinsed him thirty seconds earlier.

Beth did her patented Beth smile. I almost believed what I'd just said. She nodded like she understood not just everything but *everything* everything and she waved and she turned and she followed Harry out through the automatic doors that hissed like they were blowing kisses.

CHAPTER 24

Don't Cry Over Spilt Milk

Back at my desk, I checked my pocket for the USB drive and Jaz leant across and said, 'Anyone ever tell you how much your girlfriend looks like Emma Stone? It's cray cray.'

'She isn't my girlfriend,' I replied, not looking up from the pile of cheques in case my face might tell Jaz something I didn't want her knowing.

'Shame,' said Jaz.

And Gradual spoke. He'd appeared beside Jaz without any sound, which was really freaky because the door leading to the back corridor, like I've described, is protected by a keycode and clanks like a drunken knight. Maybe he's a ghost? Or maybe he's been sent by the gods to prevent me from robbing the bank because they've skipped to the end of the story and they realise that nothing good can ever come of breaking the law?

Either way, Gradual wasn't happy that:

1. Jaz was talking to me.
2. I hadn't finished the cheques.
3. I had a coffee.

It was really number three that vexed him the most. Checking there were no customers, he asked Jaz to explain why all food and drink was banned from the cashiers' desks.

'Really?' asked Jaz. Gradual nodded, lips painfully tight. 'Because we might spill coffee on customers and that would be bad.'

'Why else?' asked Gradual.

'Because it doesn't present the correct image.'

'Which is?'

'Professional?'

(But Jaz wasn't 100 per cent about this answer.)

'Correct. I'm vexed, Dylan. You've vexed me.'

I sighed. And he said not to sigh. And I would have told Gradual I'd seen the Queen drink coffee, and Mr Johnson, the head too, and you don't get more professional than those two. But the chance to be a smart arse was obliterated by the sudden rush of action. As I handed over the cup, its lid smoking like a gun barrel, the door clunked open and Tom, all arms and legs like a praying mantis at a rave, shot into the cramped space as Gradual turned to leave . . . holding my smoking coffee. Often when dramatic things happen people say they take place in slow motion but I saw a TV programme that said that people only *remember* things happening in slow motion. Whatever – this Saturday's calamity didn't happen in slow motion because if it had Tom or Gradual might have done something about Gradual knocking his coffee-holding hand into Tom's groin. The force of impact made Gradual squeeze the Styrofoam and the coffee erupted like angry black lava all over the front of Tom's trousers and particularly the area around his flies.

Tom, grinning, screamed. The door hadn't yet shut, and he was off down the corridor but you could hear his screaming shake the bank. It was only muffled when he entered, presumably, the toilet.

And the door closed.

'Oops,' said Jaz. 'Do you think he's okay?'

Gradual stood frozen at the moment of collision, his shoulders round and his arms tensed like he was showing off muscles he did not possess, holding the coffee cup, which was completely empty. There wasn't even a drop to stain the floor.

'Sorry,' I said because I felt like I ought to say something, even though it was 100 per cent not my fault.

Gradual shook his head very slowly. He stepped over to my desk and deposited the coffee cup there. A single tear of black coffee traced from the cup's lip. Gradual continued shaking his head. And he looked at me. I kind of thought I was going to be immediately sacked or shouted at and I think I'd rather be sacked but, instead, he said in a voice washed of emotion, 'You'd better go and see if Tom's okay.'

I nodded. Gradual opened the door. Gradual stayed with Jaz at the cashiers' desks, probably to talk about me.

I knocked with trembling knuckles at the bathroom door. I could hear movement through the wood, but there was no reaction to my knocking. I tried the handle. The door opened.

On the floor, discarded like jeans in my bedroom, were Tom's trousers. They looked like a pair of fabric pythons. The corner cubicle shook with grunting.

'Are you okay?' I said. The cubicle stopped moving. 'Tom?'

His response was shouted, his voice breaking.

'My skin's peeling off,' he said. 'It's bright red.'

'What are you doing?'

'Water,' he said. 'Cold water.'

'Do you want anything?'

'No.'

The toilet flushed in a tiny roar.

Before I turned to leave, a flash of metal winked from Tom's trousers. I knew instantly what it was: his keys. There was no decision, for as soon as I realised, I fell to my knees and crawled over. Tom must have heard the movement because he called out, 'What are you doing?'

'Putting your trousers on the dryer. They're wet through.'

I stood and lifted the heavy mass of wet, warm material, enough to make me a complete suit. The trousers left a pool of dark coffee, as if they'd scorched the floor. I swivelled the hand-dryer's head so it pointed upwards. And I lay the trousers across this metal funnel and I slapped the ON switch, over which someone had stuck a yellow smiley emoji sticker, and the room was filled with the sound of aggressive drying. And, as this was happening, I slipped Tom's keys off the belt loop.

The corridor was empty. Its lights hummed in approval.

I checked my pocket for the USB drive. It was there of course, because I'd been checking every three minutes that it was. I jogged to the end of the corridor and I couldn't help smiling as I thought that in a day's time I'd be taking Beth something a lot more special than an Americano. I'd take her a wad of cash. Maybe I'd also take something like an Americano *and* a slice of chocolate cake or one of those cookies they do in Nero with the caramel. I could afford it after all.

I was at the thin wooden door panel that protected the ATM's backside. I threw it open, checking once and twice over my shoulder that I was alone. I didn't have much time – Tom was occupied with cooling off his privates, but Gradual could emerge from the cashiers' desks at any point. If he did, which, knowing him, he would, I'm not sure how I'd explain why I was opening the back of the cash machine with stolen keys, other than by making vague reference to my made-up project. But what I needed to do would take seconds and I whispered a prayer to both Emma Stone and God for protection and good luck for once. I found the only key small enough to open the ATM's lock and when it fitted and turned easily I knew in my heart of hearts that this was my moment of victory. It felt good. Like when Crystal Palace beat Sheffield Wednesday in the last game of the season to avoid relegation to League One.

There was the keycode to go and I think I knew the combination (Clue: Tom had said 'boobs' last Saturday) but with the USB waiting patiently in my left hand and my right finger shooting like a rocket towards the first number, you wouldn't believe it but:

A LOUD ALARM SOUNDED.

CHAPTER
25

Nobody Said Robbing a Bank was Easy

All the meals I've ever eaten travelled with battery acid up my oesophagus. My heart tripled in size and pushed against my ribcage. I couldn't hear my repeated swearing and frantic breathing because of the ongoing raptor shriek of the ALARM. I slammed shut the ATM, locked it and shut the second door. I shoved the keys and USB drive back in my pocket. The ALARM continued screaming but now I realised it sounded different to last Saturday's. I took one, two steps from the ATM and there! A grey cloud like a middle-aged vaper crept from under the bathroom door. I broke into a run as Gradual stepped out from the cashiers' desks and we met at the bathroom door. Tom emerged, without his trousers on his legs but with his trousers in his hands. Amazingly the fabric was both smoking black upward trails and dripping what might have been black tears.

'My trousers caught fire,' he said. 'On the dryer.'

And his eyebrows rose like the spirits of two dead caterpillars.

Gradual didn't even say anything but walked off to his office. Shortly after, the alarm stopped sounding. He must have an override for it in there or something.

Although the trace of smoke was already dissipating like a ghost's fart, the corridor was heavy with what smelt like burnt hair. The kind of scent that sticks in your throat.

'Look,' said Tom, standing there in boxer shorts about the same size as my trousers, 'if he asks, I'm telling him it was you who put them on the dryer. This is my career, Dylan. I've worked too hard to see it flushed down the pan because of a pair of smoking trousers.'

I nodded. I took his keys from my pocket. I felt a bit sick.

'I've got your keys,' I said. 'They were on the bathroom floor. I thought you'd want them looked after because if Gradual had found them . . .'

Smiling, he took the keys and disappeared back into the bathroom.

I returned to the cashiers' desks. Jaz was talking to a man in a baseball cap. As I sat back down at the pile of cheques, my trousers pulled tight and pushed the sharp edges of the USB drive against my thigh. In RS we once heard how mad Christians sometimes wear this thing called a cilice, which bites into their skin and reminds them of sin and God and the everlasting misery of being religious. (Mr Franzen, the RS teacher, said being an RS teacher had the same effect.) The bite of the USB drive reminded me of this, reminded me of the endless lessons spent in RS, of how little time there was until Beth would be evicted from her second home of the holiday. Including today, there were nine days of the holiday left. I pulled out my phone, also tight against my thigh, and made some calculations.

9 days is 216 hours. 216 hours is 12,960 minutes. 12,960 minutes is 777,600 seconds.

Time is the ultimate cilice.

I jumped when Jaz tapped my shoulder and asked if I wanted a drink. I made like the jump was a cough and after I'd finished clearing my throat, I asked if she was joking.

'Black coffee, right?' she said.

The circles under her eyes were as dark as Darth

163

Vader's helmet, I swear, and she obviously wasn't joking.

'Won't Gradual get mad?'

She rolled her chair back from the desk and pointed down below. There were three mugs.

'You've got to be subtle,' she said. 'What he doesn't know can't hurt him.'

I *did* want a drink but I didn't want coffee. I was worried that coffee was a gateway drug to adulthood – I'd start wearing corduroys and reading the paper and dressing up in Lycra to go cycling in the countryside – so I said I was okay.

Jaz returned and handed me a steaming mug. It would have been more awkward to say I didn't want it, so I made like the enamel didn't burn my hand and quickly hid it by my feet but in a way that suggested I was totally down with drinking coffee.

Jaz sat and sipped.

'Black medicine,' she said. 'That's what the Sioux call it.'

'Who's the Sue? Does she work here in the week?'

Jaz laughed and I pretended to understand what was happening.

'I adore Native Americans,' she said. 'Like their way

of life. I know Chislehurst has the pond and the ducks, but imagine living in a tepee in Yellowstone Park.'

I went camping in Year Seven and it was the worst thing ever. All the fresh air makes you fart.

Jaz had this weird tepee and totem pole look. Thankfully she snapped out of it and asked what Gradual was making me do.

'I'm entering these cheques into Excel,' I said.

'Why?'

'Dunno.'

There must have been something going on with my face because she smiled like women older than me sometimes do. She said I was doing something right because I'd managed to last longer than most Saturday kids.

'This is my second Saturday.'

'Exactly,' and she turned to serve a customer.

I took sips as I worked. Mainly because Jaz looked over every so often to check. She thought I wanted coffee but was afraid of Gradual. Do people REALLY enjoy this stuff? Maybe it's an acquired taste. Like Buster Keaton, you just have to push on through.

A bit like robbing banks.

It's Better to Fail Before,
Rather Than During, a Crime

Something weird happened when I finished the coffee. I focused on the data entry. When I handed over the cheques and showed Gradual the completed spreadsheet, he actually smiled.

'I was in the zone,' I said.

(By smiled, I mean he pulled his lips back from his coffee-stained teeth.)

'Tom's had to go home, by the way,' he said. 'Physically he's fine, but psychologically he needs time.'

'So unfair,' said Jaz, 'getting to go home early.' She looked at the clock and did a voice like a wrestling commentator: 'But, hey! It's . . . the . . . weekend! We can go too!'

'Quite,' said Gradual and disappeared off with the cheques and netbook.

Getting up from my chair, I stretched like a Championship footballer. Before anything else, I needed a slash, so I excused myself past Jaz who was shoving stuff into her bag and saying 'Quick, quick, quick'. The toilet still had a trace of burnt trouser to the air but I didn't care. It was better than the usual smell.

As I stood at the toilet, I thought about all the sweet things I could fill the afternoon with. And of all the sweet things, going back to bed felt like the sweetest.

There was a thump, like someone's shoulder, at the room's door.

'I'm in here,' I said, but they didn't reply and they didn't try the door again.

I sorted my trousers and banged my way out of the cubicle like a broken bumper car. If I'm honest, I didn't clean my hands because, like Jaz had shouted, it was the weekend and all I wanted was to go home. Failure to install the USB lingered like B.O., but I could feel sorry for myself in bed. Mum usually bought jam doughnuts on Saturday mornings and if I installed the thing next week and withdrew the money on the same day, I might still be in time to save Beth. Even if she'd already moved

167

from the high-rise, there'd be money to rent a house somewhere nice like Bickley maybe.

When I tried the bathroom door and it didn't open, I guessed it was because I'd locked it, pulling across the silver bar through the feline instinct to keep my business to myself. And I was right, so I slid the lock free. I tried the handle again. Nothing. My mind imploded like a dying star, instantly consumed by a dark matter that understood the significance of this unmoving rectangle of wood. I turned the handle left and then right but this didn't magically solve the problem.

The problem of the locked door.

'Hey!' I shouted. 'I'm in the bathroom.'

My voice bounced about the room but from the other side of the door came silence, like the wood marked the barrier between our world and absolute nothingness. I banged with the soft flesh at the bottom of my fists. I knocked with my knuckles. I slapped full palms against the unforgiving wood. I yelled, I hollered. I whimpered a bit.

Nothing.

I turned to lean my back against the door. It felt cool. The cheap nylon of my shirt stuck against my skin. Don't panic. This isn't 1979. You have your phone. I smoothed

168

down my red tie. My phone! Yes! God bless technology. Only I didn't know who to ring. Not Beth, obviously. I opened Safari and found the bank's corporate website. I clicked through to 'locate your branch' and underneath Max Gradual's name was a telephone number.

(Was it me or was it getting hot in here?)

It clicked through to a voice. The voice told me that phone calls might be recorded for training purposes. And it rang through to another voice that gave me a few options and numbers to press. Number three was to speak to an operator, so I did that.

(This wasn't Gradual. This was a call centre.)

Classical music played. And continued playing. And continued playing. It reminded me of Thursday afternoons in Year Nine and endless music-themed assemblies, i.e. not good memories. And I paced around the space and I cursed the cups of coffee and finally a voice broke through the classical music. It was a recorded voice of a northern woman who sounded like she baked cakes and was a really good mother/might be a robot.

'Apologies for the delay in connecting you to a representative. We are currently experiencing unusually high volumes of traffic. Have you checked the website, and in particular the help section, which contains answers to many common queries? Alternatively please continue to hold.'

Mine was not a common query. I continued to hold and I sweated.

Darren's voice, louder than was comfortable, made me jump. He had a warm Irish accent.

'Hi, I'm Darren. What's your name?'

Should I answer? Yes, I decided, I should. I didn't want to be a nameless victim.

'Dylan.'

'And how may I help you today, Dylan?'

'I'm locked in the staff toilets.'

There was a click as Darren disconnected the call.

CHAPTER 27

You Don't Want to End Up Locked Away

Darren had probably thought it was a prank. Teenage boys do them: the pranks. There was a tremor to my fingers as I redialled the number and, again, was connected to a message telling me the call might be recorded. On the plus side, I wouldn't die through being locked in the toilet over the weekend.

I was trapped. Terror began to spread from my stomach to my whole body.

Did the cleaners visit? I vaguely remembered someone saying they came on a Saturday afternoon. I could hang on for a few hours, right? How long before Mum or Dad raised the alarm? This evening? Would they search here? Worst-case scenario: trapped until Monday morning. There was water. I wouldn't be forced to poo in the bin because there was a toilet. *And* Mum wouldn't be here to make me do chores.

But, Jesus, I had my phone! I'd call home! As the operator spoke through the options, I ended the call and rang Mum's phone. It went straight to voicemail. Dad's phone rang out. I called Rita. She didn't answer. I imagined her, still in bed, turning over because of the vibration of her phone and seeing it was me and silencing the thing. The more people with phones, the fewer answer them.

Should I try the bank number again? I could ring the police. Was this an emergency? How long had I been locked in here? I had a USB in my trousers with an illegal code that could hack cash machines. I didn't really want to ring the police.

My knees, like my family, failed me and I slid down the wall to my backside. My eyes flapped around the room and fell on the window THE ENTRANCE POINT OF THE PIGEONS.

I'd never be able to escape through the window; there were thick metal bars for one thing. If I were lucky, though, I might be able to lure a pigeon by opening the window. And, having lured a pigeon, the alarm might magically be triggered. Like it did that once.

How long had I been here? Minutes. You never know, the bank might not even be totally locked up yet. Grinning Tom would come grinning through and he'd release me and I'd have a grin across my face as big as his. Ah! The scrapes teenagers get in!

I turned over the plastic wastebin. Tissues flooded the floor. I carried the bin to the wall, just to the side of the sink. I stood on the bin. It squeaked, but it held. Stretching as far as my fifteen-year-old arms would reach, I managed to get a finger to the window's silver arm. I lifted it. It dropped a little on its hinges. With the plastic bin cracking further, and making a sound like a ship in a storm, I caught the window arm between my thumb and forefinger. I pushed it. The window swung open like a dream. I caught the arm on the stud and secured its position as the bin gave way and I tumbled to the floor in a thunder-crack of plastic. The four sides of the bin had spread out, breaking along the edges, and looking like a blossoming flower. My backside hurt only slightly. My forehead was wet with sweat.

I looked to the window. It was definitely open but there was no pigeon. Yet. Birds, like banks, need time.

My phone rang. I pulled it out. Dad.

'Dylan,' he said. 'It's Dad.'

'I know,' I said.

'You called.'

He sounded out of breath. It was unlike Dad to sound out of breath. Not because he was fit – the opposite: he never did any exercise. But I wasn't going to worry about details like this. How was I going to break the news? Which words would I use to explain my situation and minimise the likelihood of getting in trouble? It's the curse of being a teenager: whenever/however you get in trouble, you're always the one to be blamed.

'They locked me in the bank,' I said. 'And they've all gone home.'

Dad made a strange noise down the phone. Halfway between a yawn and a groan.

'Right,' he said. 'And you don't have the keys?'

'No,' I said. 'It's a bank.'

'Have you got the manager's number?'

'No,' I said.

'Always get your boss's number,' said Dad because he never misses an opportunity to offer advice.

'What should I do?' I asked.

'Wait a sec.'

There was a rustling noise. I heard Dad's voice, muffled, calling out to Mum.

'Dylan's locked in his bank,' he said. 'Wants to know what to do.' I couldn't make out Mum's reply, but Dad answered, 'Yeah, I told him that. He doesn't have them, though.'

The phone croaked and Dad's voice returned nice and loud.

'Whereabouts in the bank are you?'

'I'm in the toilet. It's right at the back. There's a window with bars on it.'

'And you can't squeeze out of that?'

'There are bars on it.'

'Okay. Look, Dylan. You hold tight. And we'll get it sorted. Don't you panic.'

'I'm not.'

Dad said bye. I said bye. And the conversation ended.

One thing I'd learnt while working at the bank was that when you're an adult you spend a lot of time waiting. Jaz spent her life waiting for the weekend to come round, so she could go out raving. Tom probably spent time waiting for the chance to go to comedy clubs, so people wouldn't ask about his constant grinning. Even Gradual was probably waiting for a promotion to a bank made out of stone and closer to central London, a place where he didn't have to deal with people like me. But ambitious branch managers need to check their toilets before locking up, even though I wouldn't have put it past him to imprison me on purpose. He'd spin the situation to provide ammunition when it came to firing me.

'And remember that time that you locked yourself in the toilet?' he'd say. 'We can't be employing people who lock themselves in toilets.'

I waited as seconds turned to minutes. The smell of burnt trouser drifted around me.

I went on Facebook. No updates from anyone interesting. Not even Beth. Mum had reposted a cartoon about the Prime Minister, which might have been funny if I understood it. Nothing on Twitter. Palace had zero to offer. Should I tweet the bank's customer services?

Locked in your toilets. Plz send help.

No. Beth might read it. Or, worse, Harry.

I checked the branch account. The last tweet was one from a year ago, advertising a charity medieval day. If I survived today, I should volunteer to run the social media.

'I'll make some sick memes,' I'd tell Gradual. 'Sick. Memes.'

The phone battery read 48 per cent, which sucked because I'd charged it overnight and had used it, like, once in the morning. Times are troubling when you engage low-power mode, which is what I was now forced to do.

A flutter of wings. A soft cooing. I looked to the window. Get in! A pigeon!

(I named him 'Peter', bringer of freedom.)

'Peter,' I said, looking at him and smiling.

In the blink of an eye a hand appeared at the window, caught Peter's legs and Peter disappeared back from where he'd come, leaving no feathers but a troubled squawk. And then a face, appeared in stages – its owner was obviously climbing a ladder.

'Dylan Thomas?' said the face.

Never Be Too Proud to Ask for Help

Without being able to see his uniform I could tell it belonged to a fireman. He had fireman's eyes. Not the round, caring eyes of Fireman Sam but the tiny rocks that spend half their time admiring a muscular body through a phone's front-facing camera.

Before I could reply the bank's alarm started. The fireman fell, his face disappearing from the frame.

I moved closer and shouted. 'I am Dylan!'

And a thumb appeared, pointing skyward. This was replaced by another face, but this one I recognised: Dad's.

He was smiling like isn't all this funny, like he'd had one too many coffees, like he'd never met Gradual, which he hadn't, like he didn't plan to rob a bank, which he didn't. As far as I knew.

His mouth moved. I couldn't hear its words. The alarm, as it had been with the first pigeon, was so loud that it didn't emerge from one particular place, but ranged across time and space. It penetrated your body like an X-ray. Dad gave up trying to communicate. The fireman took his place. It was like a crap puppet show, this swapping of faces. But now the fireman had a tool and a yellow helmet with a protective face screen. I recognised his tool from the DT workshop. It was an angle grinder. With the arrival of not only my dad but also the angle grinder I felt that dull turning of my stomach that indicated I was so going to be in trouble. And sooner rather than later. But what had I done wrong? Gone to the toilet? Was that a crime nowadays? Should I have told someone? Why? *They* locked *me* in here. That I was planning to rob the bank had nothing to do with it. Forget about the whole bank-robbing thing. I was the victim.

With a fat glove, angle-grinder man waved me back. I checked the USB drive in my pocket. Should I put it up my bum? No joke. Drug dealers do it all the time. But with drugs, not USB drives, even though USB drives have got smaller. There was a chance that the authorities, whoever they might be and no doubt already pooling outside in their uniforms and shiny cars, might ask me to empty my pockets. What if they found the USB? What if they accessed its contents? That was probably beyond Dad's technical capabilities, but the police had ICT divisions filled with spotty maths geeks. The thing about my internal cavities is they wouldn't be searched. Not until the police station, at least.

On reflection, I decided to keep my bum empty. I already had a stomach ache and I didn't want to provoke my body further by sticking metal where it shouldn't be stuck. So I stood against the far wall as the fireman took the angle grinder to the first of three iron bars that protected the window. White sparks splashed like quality inside fireworks. He cut through the metal like urine through snow. Bottom. Top. And the bar fell into the bathroom. He'd done well to only leave a stub of the same thickness of a couple of 2p pieces. Maybe he was a DT teacher in real life? He didn't have the face of a DT teacher. He only had one chin. And the second bar went the same way as the first and so did the third. And the alarm continued yelling. The fireman dropped out of sight. Surely the alarm would be registered by central office? Surely Gradual would be summoned to silence the thing? Think of the local residents, and their Saturday-afternoon Pimm's being disturbed. It was an outrage.

How long had I been trapped? Half an hour? And I'd not asked anyone to cut through the metal bars. I'd not asked anyone to do anything. It must have been Dad who'd called the fire brigade. Not me. I'd make sure I told Gradual that. I'd been preparing to wait the thing out like a proper little trooper.

When the fireman next appeared at the window he wasn't wearing his protective helmet and he wasn't holding an angle grinder. He folded a rough sack, the type you might store potatoes in if you lived on a farm a hundred years ago, across the bottom of the window frame, covering the bars' stumps. And a bit like Rapunzel, he let a fold-up ladder drop and it unrolled like a carpet, the thin metal bars striking the floor. It was difficult to climb because it was flush with the wall and the rungs were pencil thin, but I pulled myself up until he gripped my wrists. What I now experienced must have been what being born feels like. Head first, I was pulled into a new world, a world of sunshine, and an anxious waiting father. I didn't think I would pass through the window space and, if I were a centimetre wider in circumference, I wouldn't have. But the fit was as perfect as the video tape that Mr Brown, our Year Seven History teacher, slotted into his antique VCR player to show us an episode of *Blackadder* as a treat at the end of every half-term.

The fireman carried me under his arm like a cat from a tree. He planted me on the tarmac at the back of the bank and I could smell the bins and their rotting vegetables that had come from who knows where, not the bank. Dad stood there thanking the fireman and not smelling much better than the bins and telling me to thank the men too. I'd hardly taken in the scene, a red fire engine, its chrome catching the sun, two other fire officers, one drinking a can of Coke and the other on her phone, the bins, a random kid on his bike, gawping, before Gradual appeared on his motorbike, the engine drowned out by the continuing alarm.

'Who's this?' shouted the fireman.

The gawping kid cycled off.

'The manager,' I replied, shouting.

CHAPTER 29

Expect to Fail and You Won't Be Disappointed

Gradual jumped from his bike and, in the same motion, had his Iron Man crash helmet off.

'What's going on?' he shouted.

The bike toppled over. There was some fussing about to get it upright. When this was done, the fireman explained he'd rescued me from the bank toilet. And he indicated the ladder and the window as if to provide proof in case Gradual didn't believe him.

'Why didn't you just call me?' shouted Gradual to the fireman. 'Why employ the heavy machinery?'

'An angle grinder isn't heavy machinery, sir. And we've had reports of the bank's alarm sounding on and off for weeks now. *And* there was an agoraphobic minor in distress. That's why, sir.'

Gradual stabbed his eyes at me.

'Thomas?'

Although he only uttered my surname, I took the word to mean that he wanted to kill me. He looked at the ladder and the window. He had the same expression as you'd expect if he'd just been told that his whole life had been a lie and he was actually an android with six hours remaining before his batteries ran out forever.

'Let me turn off the alarm and we can talk about the damage.'

But when Gradual returned, the fire engine had gone. They'd left a leaflet called 'EMERGENCY SERVICES AND DAMAGE: A DUMMY'S GUIDE'. Dad handed it over but Gradual didn't seem interested. Standing in an alarm-free Saturday afternoon, with the sounds of suburban London humming gently in the background, Gradual, in his biker's leathers, wanted to know 'who the flip' Dad was.

'Are you his carer?' he asked.

Dad laughed.

'You could say that,' he said. 'I am his father.'

These last three words silenced Gradual. There were heavy *Star Wars* feels. Whatever he'd planned to say caught in his throat and seemed to choke him because his face went purple.

'Sorry about the window,' I said.

(It was now shut. Gradual had closed it when disabling the alarm.)

But he wasn't worried about all that. Instead he coughed up a question. 'Thomas's father?'

'Dylan's father. Kay Thomas. How's it going?'

And Dad offered his hand and Gradual shook it. Slowly.

'Right,' said Gradual. His head turned from Dad to me to Dad to me. Cogs turned in his head. Desperate, oily cogs. A smile flashed across his face, revealing the coffee-coloured teeth. A smile a snake would offer a mouse. If snakes could smile. 'That makes things a lot easier. Dylan here said you'd passed.'

Dad blinked. 'Passed what?'

'Passed away.'

My voice, a mouse's, if mice could speak, said it had been Rita who'd told Gradual that Dad, and Mum, had died.

'Rita?' asked Dad, whose constant questions were beginning to wear. 'Dead or alive, Mr Gradual, I've been meaning to talk to you about Dylan's job here. About him getting locked up. About the pigeon.'

Gradual nodded like he truly understood. Involuntarily my buttocks tensed. I was about to get sacked. Maybe even shouted at. And in front of Dad. Maybe I could silence them if I revealed my only motivation behind all this was to rob the bank?

'You're not going to believe this,' said Gradual, his teeth lingering and the coffee 'smile' looking about as natural as a polar bear in Plumstead. 'But I'm meant to be on a horse right now. Jousting. Ten minutes ago, in fact. It's something I do. Medieval re-enactments. Of course, I'll have to abandon all those plans. What with this.' He motioned to the bank. The memory of what he next did still wakes me in a cold sweat. *He put a hand on my shoulder, a clammy hand.* 'Dylan, why don't you come down to the bank at, say eight thirty Monday morning, before we've opened, and you can bring Dad or Mum with you. I'll answer any questions any of you might have. And we can have a good chat about how you came to be locked in the toilet and all the other tiny, troubling things that have happened since you started working here. How about that?'

The suggestion was framed as a question and if it had been a question, I'd have definitely said no.

'Great,' said Dad. 'I'll be at work but my wife'll come.'

(Dad was *never* at work at eight thirty. He stayed in bed because he said it made sense to wait for the traffic to die down.)

186

'Fantastic,' said Gradual. I didn't like his fake friendliness. It was unsettling. I'd have preferred an old-style shouting. 'Good to meet you, Mr Thomas. You'll have to excuse me. I've a building to secure.'

'Did he say medieval re-enactments?' asked Dad as we watched Gradual go. 'He should install a portcullis.'

CHAPTER
30

The Darkest Point of the Night Comes Before Sunrise
(or something like that)

Mum insisted I wear my white shirt, red tie and black trousers. She said it was important to look professional. Okay, she was wearing her running kit but this wasn't a morning for argument. Not with Mum and not with Gradual. It was a morning for sucking it up, for chewing down on whatever might be served, regardless of taste. If there were a filament of a chance I could have one more Saturday at the bank, the last before school started again, I might still be able to get the code on the cash machine, steal the money and save Beth. Because I wasn't sacked yet. I was still alive. And with Mum on my side, who knows what might happen?

(I wasn't convinced.)

Tightening my tie in the mirror, I felt like I was dressing for a funeral.

'Let's get the facts straight,' said Mum, in the car. 'This manager has you catching wild animals. Refuses you coffee. Sets you pointless data-entry tasks. Locks you in toilets. We should email our MP. We should tweet the papers.'

I told Mum that while all those things happened, they were all also kind of my fault. Apart from the pigeon. And I also asked what the smell was because, to be honest, it was making me feel dead-cat sick.

'That's potpourri,' she said. 'To disguise the sweat and Big Macs after your sister and her friends borrowed the car.'

'I don't like my job and I don't think I'm going to go any more,' I said.

Mum stared her Superman laser eyes and almost crashed into an Audi. She said the point of jobs was not liking them. The only people who like their jobs are people rich enough not to work.

'And you're not getting sacked because if there's one thing I've learnt from the call centre, it's never to take no for an answer. You've got to imagine the customer is a bone and you're the dog. If you manage to get your teeth in, they've no chance.'

Mum made a growling noise. It was cringe.

'You've not met Max Gradual.'

She snorted. Maybe things weren't as desperate as I'd thought. Mum can be end-of-level boss formidable when she wants. There was a Geography teacher in Year Nine who never marked our books and after a ten-minute meeting with Mum, you should have seen the red ink across our work the very next day. He probably had to buy an ink factory to keep supplied. He also left school at the end of the year. Which had nothing to do with the meeting with Mum.

'If you had ten thousand pounds,' I said, 'what would you do with it?'

Gradual was delivering the morning briefing as I tapped on the bank's automatic doors. Mum circled her eyes with her hands like she was holding invisible binoculars, pushing against the glass to get a look.

'Who does he think he is?' she asked. 'Mr Motivator?'

I didn't ask who Mr Motivator was. He sounded like a crap superhero.

Mum attacked the glass doors with open palms. They shivered, almost in fear. The heads of the bank employees turned as Gradual waved acknowledgement, gave a final few words of 'encouragement', and stepped over to unlock the entrance. There were three other bank workers. There stood Tom, basketball tall and grinning. There was also a man with a hipster beard and a sofa stomach and a woman with huge hair. Jaz was probably in bed 'coming down'.

'Why's the tall man grinning?' asked Mum.

After shaking Mum's hand, but not mine, Gradual suggested we follow him to his office. I'd not been allowed in before now, but the space was exactly as I imagined it: cramped, functional and windowless. A filing cabinet in the corner, a desk too large for the room, a freestanding fan. The walls were bare apart from a motivational poster showing a sunrise over Canary Wharf and the text I HAD A DREAM – MARTIN LUTHER KING. In the wall space behind Gradual's desk was a framed degree certificate from a uni I'd not heard of. His subject? Economics.

Gradual pulled up two plastic chairs and told us to sit down, then squeezed through the space between the wall and his desk to do the same. That his desktop was completely empty, apart from a thin computer screen, didn't mean he was organised. It meant he never did any work. When he sat down his leather bank manager's chair squeaked out a fart.

(I hid my grin with a fake cough.)

'I'd offer you a tea,' he said. 'But I've nobody to make it!'

I think this was an attempt to lighten the mood. I sat there with my hands in my lap and my head lowered. I'd never actually been sent to the head teacher's office, but this was how I'd be sitting if I had.

'I want what I'm about to say to be positive,' he said. 'I've said this many times but everyone makes mistakes in life. It's how you react to them that makes the difference.'

(How many kids had there been before me?)

'I want to talk about the pigeon.'

Gradual had been all smiles and soft eyebrows until this point, but at Mum's interruption, there was a glimpse of his true character. His face hardened and his smile wavered.

'In a moment,' he said. 'But first I think it's important that you, both of you, hear what I have to say. Having reviewed your time with us so far, Dylan, I'm not sure it's working out. I'm sure you'd agree—'

'A pigeon is a wild animal,' said Mum. 'It carries diseases. I googled.'

'Okay,' said Gradual. 'If we could move away from the pigeon for a second.'

192

'Histoplasmosis is a respiratory disease that may be fatal.'

'Putting . . .' Gradual struggled to say 'histoplasmosis'.

'Histoplasmosis,' said Mum.

'Putting histoplasmosis aside for just one moment—'

'I had to wash my son's trousers three times before the stains came out. Three times.'

'Yes,' said Gradual. He interlinked his fingers and leant forward, his forearms flush with the desk. His chair squeaked again. 'I hear what you're saying. But the truth is, Mrs Thomas—'

'The truth?' said Mum. 'The truth is you locked my son in the toilets and he had to be rescued by the fire brigade. Can you imagine the stress that caused him? He's fourteen years old. He's fragile.'

'Fifteen,' I said.

Gradual looked at me. His tongue darted from his mouth to moisten his lips. He returned his glance to Mum.

'Perhaps if Dylan would like to step out for a second . . .'

Mum's eyes reddened. 'There's no reason—'

'Mum,' I said. I placed a hand on her tracksuited leg. What I meant by saying 'Mum' was that she didn't

193

need to get worked up on my behalf but she understood that I meant I wanted to leave.

'How about you wait outside?' suggested Gradual but looking at Mum. 'We'll call when we're done with the adult talk, Thomas.' He shook his head. 'Dylan, I mean. Sorry.'

CHAPTER 31

Take Advantage of Unexpected Opportunities

Stepping from the office, I closed the door quietly. At the end of the corridor, on his hands and knees, Tom was loading an ATM. And I wasn't surprised because this was always going to happen and not just because it was the morning after a weekend of withdrawals but because I was sure God had planned this scene to tease me.

Thanks, God. Nice one. You suck.

I didn't call out to Tom. I leant against the wall. No sound bled from the office door and I couldn't be bothered to put my ear to the wood. I'd only get caught. The summer had been a succession of moments of getting caught.

I wanted to be anywhere but here. On the computer,

researching Vietnam. Even Orpington McDonald's was preferable. I got my phone out. Like you do when you're waiting in dimly lit corridors. Nothing was happening, no matter how frantically I refreshed the social media apps or BBC Sport.

'Hey, man, I thought you were getting fired.'

Tom, grinning, was craning his diplodocus neck. The corridor possessed the eerie threat of the corridors in *The Shining*. All long and creepy with something gross at the far end.

'My mum's in there,' I said in a stage whisper. 'With Gradual.'

'Your mum—' called Tom like he was about to say something offensive and inappropriate but thought better of it for once because, you know, I'm a kid.

He pulled himself to his knees and, even without half of his leg length, he was taller than me.

I wouldn't like to be tall. You'd not be able to hide anywhere. That said, all the girls in my year fancied John Perkins and he had nothing going for him apart from his height.

'You couldn't do me one last solid? No hard feelings about telling Gradual how you set my trousers on fire, yeah? Sweet.'

I was about to tell him to forget it and to grin while doing so. I calculated, however, using my impressive calculating powers, that he was sitting at an open ATM and what I wanted pretty much more than anything else in the world was an open ATM, so . . .

'What?' I asked, walking the length of the corridor to join him.

'You couldn't watch this bad boy while I fetch another cartridge, would you? I haven't woken up yet. Nice one.' I was saying yes before he'd finished asking. 'And don't get any funny ideas about taking money. I've not opened the packages yet.'

I stuttered and stammered as he pulled himself to his full height, like some kind of wizard revealing his true powerful form. He half slapped, half punched my shoulder and it really hurt but I didn't complain because –

'Nah, I'm only pranking you. Take as much money as you want! No. I'm joking again. The machine keeps a track of its contents. Unlike your mum. Yeah. So.'

He made for the door to the cashiers' windows.

'What does that even mean?' I called after him, acting completely chill.

Without turning, he opened out his pterodactyl arms

and shrugged. As he passed through to the cashiers' desks, the door shut with a thud of approval.

I fell to my knees and, as I did, I felt an almighty pain and it wasn't the thin carpet against my legs but it was the thought-fear that I might not have the USB drive.

But, celebrate being a teenage boy, because I hadn't taken the drive out of my trousers since Saturday. That's how I roll. And even as I was thinking all this I could feel the sharp contours of the USB drive against my thigh like it was desperate to be deployed. I pulled it out, located the USB slot, nudged the trailing cords out of the way and successfully inserted the drive. Well, not on my first attempt because who ever inserts a USB the right way round on their first attempt?

Fifteen seconds. That's the minimum the instructions said to keep the drive inserted. You *could* leave it in forever. Or fifteen minutes. Or whatever. But fifteen seconds was the minimum needed for the code to work its magic. And, like my school reports always say, I was happy with the minimum. *And* my plan stated I shouldn't leave the USB plugged in because it was best to leave a crime scene clean, so: fifteen seconds it was. Like when you're performing a hard reset and you have to keep your finger on the power button for fifteen seconds. Fifteen seconds. A quarter of a minute. Leave no trace.

Fifteen seconds lasted forever (the theory of relativity) but I wasn't going to be interrupted, not by anyone . . . Well, maybe Beth because it was all on her that I was doing this, but not Mum, not Tom, and definitely not Gradual. Fifteen seconds. I counted it under my breath, my life compressed.

How would Tom react if he caught me?

One Mississippi. Two Mississippi. Three Mississippi. What if Gradual came out and asked what I was doing? I'd be in trouble. Police trouble. I must have missed three Mississippis thinking there. Let's start again on seven. Eight Mississippi. Nine Mississippi. I needed a slash, even though I'd not drunk anything this morning. My bladder was scared, that's what it was. Imagine if I wet myself. Silver lining: it would distract from the hack code. That's what I'd do if interrupted. Yes, I'd wet myself and start crying. Got to be at twelve Mississippi by now. Thirteen Mississippi. Fourteen Mississippi. Fifteen Mississippi.

And one for luck. Check over your shoulder, no sign of Gradual's door opening. Mum once talked without stopping throughout an FA Cup semi-final. They'd be some time yet, right?

Nothing obvious changed in the innards of the ATM. The wires, the plastic, they didn't move. There were no red flashing lights, now that hack mode had been initiated. *If* it had been initiated. What if I'd not left it in long enough? I'd give it a few more seconds.

Or should I try again? No time for the old in and out. It might mess everything up. I should have printed the instructions. No, I should pull it out. Pull it out now. But . . .

CHAPTER 32

Flexibility Can Be as Important
as Detailed Planning

'What are you doing?'

Above me loomed the beard. And there was proper sweat on my forehead. Like I'd been caught by a lawn sprayer. How had I not heard the beard's approach? How did everyone here move so quietly? They must get training. I should get my ears tested. I should stop using earphones. Maybe they had special shoes?

'Looking after the cash machine. Tom forgot a cartridge. He's gone to get one.'

The beard nodded as the beard absorbed the information. The beard didn't say anything about how my voice wavered. The beard didn't say anything about the USB drive in the machine, as obvious as a wasp at a picnic. There I was, on my hands and knees like I was doing an impression of a Labrador. Should I wet myself? I'd cock a leg against the open access panel. I'd bark. That *had* been the plan if interrupted. They'd think me crazy and send me home. But I no longer needed a wee. Curse my contrary bladder.

'Your name is?'

'Dylan Thomas.'

His beard rolled into a laugh.

'Like the poet? Pretentious much?'

'Leave him alone,' said Tom, his steady voice following the slam of the cashiers' door. 'He's doing me a solid.'

Tom was my knight in shining armour, holding a cash-machine cartridge instead of a lance. I was a princess and total bae. And at least I knew the code would get installed now, seeing how the USB drive was inserted for ever more and I was sure that wasn't a problem because nobody would ever notice it. I was only going to remove it after fifteen seconds to be on the safe side. Okay, the engineer or whoever would *eventually* find it but the code deletes itself. There was nothing incriminating on the drive and by the time of its discovery, I'd be in the sixth-form, if I get the grades.

'You can't be leaving Welsh poets with open cash

machines,' said the beard. 'I'm going to have to tell Max about this. There are rules for a reason, Tom.'

'How about you tell Max about this?'

Tom offered the beard a middle finger.

But before the conversation could escalate Gradual appeared. The beard slunk off back to the cashiers' desks. Tom told Gradual he was filling up the external cash machine and everything was cool. Gradual told him to get on with it, then, and asked if I might step into his office for a second. I didn't even look at the USB as I went. Mum was still sitting. She gave me a Mum smile. Gradual squeezed back to his own seat. It farted again, a chipmunk squeak, as he sat down.

'Your mother and I,' he said, his voice a monotone as if Mum had drained him of all emotion, 'we've had a really productive chat. And, bearing in mind what she said about your sister, I'm prepared to give you a final chance. Okay, Dylan? One more go of it. Don't let me down.'

The shining joy of finally getting the hack code installed was rusted a bit by Gradual now saying I could keep the job. Because I didn't want the job. I didn't need the job. I only ever wanted the job to get access to the USB slot.

I stood. What I was about to say deserved to be said

standing up, especially as I was speaking off the top of my head, propelled by the USB triumph.

'Mr Gradual, I've not been able to sleep for the last two weeks because of nightmares about pigeons. I'll never be able to go to Trafalgar Square again. And I reckon I'm claustrophobic now, having been locked in the toilet on Saturday, so no flights or living in flats for me. I'll never be able to go to America. So, in conclusion, I don't want your job and I don't want a final chance. You're a bully and if Mum and Dad have ever taught me anything, it's that you should stand up to bullies. Sorry. Thank you anyway.' The words poured in a torrent. I felt endorphins flushing through my system, that same heightened state of being you get after a good game of *FIFA*. I pulled off my tie, freeing my neck from a hangman's noose, and pulled out my security card. I placed the two items on to Gradual's desk. Mum blinked. Gradual gawped. 'Okay?'

'I think we're done here,' said Mum, standing.

Eventually Gradual said he'd show us out.

The corridor was empty, the cash machine closed up. Tom hadn't discovered the USB. Because why would he? The slot was right at the edge of the machine, disguised by trailing wires. You'd only see the stick, the size of a fingertip, if you were looking for it.

At the automatic doors an old woman in a bobble hat knocked on the glass and pointed at her watch. Wordlessly Gradual unlocked the doors. The old woman moaned that she was too old to be made to wait outside, austerity or no. She'd lived through the seventies, for heaven's sake.

Mum didn't say anything until we got into the car. She didn't start the engine and I braced myself for the hugest telling-off of my life. How dare I speak to an adult like that? How dare I turn down a job, knowing how little money we had and how my own mother had been in the man's office pleading for him to give me a second chance? How dare I?

But Mum didn't tell me off.

'Dylan,' she said, 'I don't think you're a kid any more.'

She nodded with significance and turned the ignition.

'What did you say about Rita?'

'I said she was adopted. And was having acceptance issues that resulted in her fantasising about my death.'

'Wow.'

'Sometimes,' said Mum, 'situations call for a white lie. For the greater good. That's another thing I learnt at the call centre. Just don't tell Rita. You know what she gets like.'

Mum was right. About the lies. And about how Rita

gets. But especially about me not being a kid any more. Because kids don't successfully install USB hack codes on to cash machines, you know what I mean?

'Have you tried Burger King?' she said. 'On the high street?'

I told Mum I'd pick up an application form.

It was Monday morning. I had twelve hours to enter the hack PIN.

(And it really wasn't a problem that I'd left the USB drive in the cash machine. No problem at all. *Really*.)

CHAPTER

33

A Journey of a Thousand Miles
Begins with a Single Step

I spent the day in my bedroom, willing time to speed up. No matter how often I looked at my phone, it was always the same time: too early to try the hack. Because the bank needed to be solidly closed up before I dared entering 1842, the secret code to fortune and glory.

I got two messages – one from a friend back from Spain, wanting to know if I'd read anything for English and, if so, were we meant to make notes, and one from Pizza Hut, telling me about a sweet new meal deal. I sent one message, WhatsApping what flowed from my mind. Straight to Beth.

Coffee tonight?

Instantly, and I mean instantly, she replied:

Maybe ice cream? 👩 *Where?*

Outside Chis Costa. Next to bank. 🐬

(If I know anything about girls, it's they love emojis.)

Directors like to film during the golden hour. This is the time just after sunrise or just before sunset when the light is soft and red and makes the world seem like it could be magical after all. I'd grabbed my sports bag, told uninterested parents I was going out for a jog, promised Rita I wouldn't get arrested, and off I'd gone. Just like that. The first few steps were perfect, I wasn't even that anxious. And then the toes of my right foot caught against the half-circle grave marker of next-door's cat and I flew through the air. For a second, the flight felt liberating. Too soon gravity came pulling at my face. My chin hit the pavement with a sickening thud.

The first thing I checked was for witnesses. All it takes is a nearby iPhone to have an accident become a viral sensation. Luckily the street was empty. I pulled myself up and inspected the damage. My knees ached a little and my chin felt as if someone had taken a cheese grater to it. I touched it with a fingertip and it hurt and felt sticky. My finger came back with something like a blob of raspberry jam.

I thought about turning back but between Mum's

fussing and Rita's mocking, I thought it best to grit my teeth, even if the action tightened my skin and made my chin hurt even more. And, anyway, I could still walk. Bane broke Batman's back and the Dark Knight still managed to get through his to-do list.

So I walked the grey streets of suburbia with the bus stops and polite front lawns and, despite being able to feel my pulse through my chin, I thought that everything might turn out all right in the end. And then a 51 passed and as the bus changed gear it coughed black smoke that swirled into the form of a huge bat, which might have been warning me to turn back before it was too late.

If alarms started ringing the moment I entered the code, maybe the police wouldn't imagine anyone could be so stupid as to rob a bank just a short walk away from their house. I had that going for me. I'd pretend to be confused. I could wet myself to add to the effect. And my chin would help with the image.

And it was like I was experiencing the world through VR goggles. Everything was *almost* real. This feeling meant I wasn't as nervous as you'd expect. And, anyway, I knew my luck too well – the most likely outcome was the code not working.

No, Dylan! PMA! Visualise the cash machine spewing all

of its lovely banknotes into your bag. Visualise paying for the most expensive Magnum ice cream with a fifty-pound note.

'Ice cream is for closers,' I'd say to Beth, hoping she got the reference to *Glengarry Glen Ross*, another story about a robbery, because it would make me appear cultured and intelligent. She'd laugh and put her arm through mine. She'd rest her head on my shoulder. She'd let me look at her History coursework. We'd laugh together.

If the code didn't work, I could use my own money, in the form of Saturday wages, to buy Beth a Cornetto or a cheap coffee or whatever. Because you've always got to have a Plan B.

My legs delivered me to Chislehurst High Street. And so, almost before I had time to prepare, the bank presented itself. And, good news, it looked dead and dark and empty. The cash machine was set facing the road, offering no protection from passing eyes. There was a woman and a child at it.

I checked my phone. Ten minutes until Beth. About three hours before the hack window closed. No new alerts.

She'd better not bring Harry.

A person from behind said, 'Take your time, fam.'

The voice broke the paralytic fear that I might be at the point of winning. The woman and child had moved from the ATM without me noticing. The machine stood free, all smeared touchscreen and curved plastic and waiting. It winked colours. I looked over my shoulder to where a proper lad with an extreme haircut eyeballed me.

'You go ahead,' I said, making like I was struggling with my wallet.

'Maybe take your card out beforehand?' said the haircut, taking my place.

'Sorry,' I said and stepped away.

You know what – I almost wanted to be caught. I almost wanted a police officer to appear at my elbow and read me my rights. It'd kind of be a relief. If the ATM code worked, it worked. And if it didn't, it didn't. You know? Like, really. But if it did work, it meant danger. It meant a different story. It meant decisions.

But . . . it also meant money.

The guy finished. He sucked his teeth as he passed.

Now I was alone. There weren't even any cars on the road. Perfect. I dropped the bag at my feet and unzipped it, pulling the opening wide enough to easily swallow the cash that would soon be pouring from the machine.

And then . . . instant panic – what's the PIN?

I took a long breath, designed to calm, because I knew I knew the PIN.

1842.

The screen flashed an advert for home insurance. I closed my eyes and visualised a smiling walk home with no police handcuffs or crying parents. There'd be a bag full of cash on my shoulder, and butterflies in the air, a coffee in my hand and Beth by my side. And it felt . . . wrong. The butterflies in my stomach turned to moths in my bowels.

Still, I was here now.

I checked over my shoulder again. There was nobody there, nobody in Chislehurst, nobody in south London, nobody. The Universe was empty, waiting only for the magic number to be entered into this cash machine.

1842 – one-fingered I entered the code and . . .

CHAPTER 34

Don't Let Your Ego Blind You to Your Plan's Faults

. . . nothing happened.

'Hmm,' I said.

The screen continued to display details of home insurance, a cartoon cottage, some percentages. Had I missed the deadline? No. Twelve hours. It wasn't even nine yet. I was well within the window. I tried again. A different finger. 1842. Nothing. One more time. 1842. No reaction.

This is the way the story ends.

Not with a bang but a whimper.

But sometimes whimpers are nicer than bangs. When you hug a puppy it whimpers.

I had a sudden vision of me at the ATM trying to steal

thousands of pounds. Only it wasn't me. It was my evil twin. And you could tell by his goatee.

What had I been thinking?

1842. I tried one more time. But this time, if I'm honest, I was hoping nothing happened. And it didn't. And I was kind of relieved.

Because, what the hell, I'd nearly robbed a bank. And I'd seen *The Shawshank Redemption*; I knew the score.

There was always my Saturday money. I could still afford to buy Beth a strawberry split with honest cash, earned through good old-fashioned elbow grease, which was a phrase Mum always used and I've never been 100 per cent sure what it actually means. I found my debit card, slid it in, entered my PIN: 1990. I tried for ten pounds.

Insufficient funds, the screen said. My card was returned.

I'm not too proud to admit there were now tears in my eyes, the same tears I'd have expected when the code hadn't worked.

'Hey, D. Sorry I'm early.'

Beth. With her hand up in greeting. Relaxed and smiling or wincing because the sun was in her eyes. And I didn't even have time to digest what had just happened apart from the immediate problem here, which was: I STILL HAD NO MONEY.

She was in running gear, looking as fresh as whipped cream and not sweating but glowing and with her hair tied back looking even more like Emma Stone than Emma Stone.

'Hey,' I said.

Seeing Beth had a particular physical effect – my chest tingled. My headache lifted. My bowels tightened. I quickly moved my hand to cradle my chin, to make like I was having a good think.

'Are you okay?' she asked, pursed lips. 'Your chin.'

I fingered the graze and smiled. 'Oh, this? It's nothing. I fell over a gravestone. So you're training for the marathon?'

She squinted. Gave me the 'you're so funny' look.

'The Chislehurst Half. I'm raising money for a charity that helps people to cope with fire or burglary without insurance. Will you sponsor me?'

I tried robbing a bank and Beth signed up to run a marathon. Spot the difference. I mean, was I really a bad person? Do evil people think they're good? I bet they do.

'Yes.' I spoke too quickly and it made me sound like

a stalker. There was an awkward pause. 'But I don't have any money.'

'Is it coffee time, then?' she asked, blinking into the sun. 'I mean Costa's closed but we could get a Diet Coke and feed the ducks or . . .' In the distance I heard the rumble of a motorcycle. I knew what I *should* do. I knew I *should* tell Beth the truth. About being an idiot.

'Why don't we just sit?' I said. 'I'm not thirsty.'

'Because of your chin?'

I didn't know whether Beth was joking or not, so I just nodded. And the motion made me wince.

We walked over to Chislehurst Common. The pond was empty, the water still like glass. Our bench had a golden rectangle screwed to it, with what had once been a name and dates. Years of tired backs had rubbed the detail away, though, and the letters were too smudged to make out.

Here, on the damp wood of the old seat, I confessed. The threatening notes to elderly women in post offices, the dead cat, the hack code, everything.

And, while doing so, I had another one of those weird out-of-body experiences and Beth listened with a perfectly round mouth of amazement.

Who was this idiot confessing to attempted bank robbery? Could it really be me?

A fox had attacked a bin. In front of us crisp packets and used nappies circled the black plastic container. Maybe I should pick the rubbish up? It'd be my first step to becoming a good person.

'I knew something was weird when you got a job in the bank,' said Beth. 'The only logical explanation was that you were planning to rob the place.'

I didn't ask if she actually meant this.

She reached across and grabbed my hand. I almost slid to the floor, like her touch had melted me. For a second, with the softness of Beth's grip and the freshness of her smile and the relief of the confession, it was like I'd taken off an iron cloak; everything felt . . . well, if not good, then normal. And there's a lot to be said for normal.

'Thanks,' I said.

'For what?'

'For not judging me.'

'That's okay. And, you know, I *did* tell you the fire wasn't your fault.'

'I thought you were just saying that.'

She squeezed my hand.

'Oh, Dylan,' she said.

(And if this were a film, if we'd been adults, we might have kissed. And . . . I think I'd have liked that.)

Instead Beth let go and stood up. She told me I was an idiot. A massive idiot. There was more to life than money. She said I could have been arrested. What had I been thinking? My fingerprints, both literal and metaphorical, were over everything. How had I ever decided all this was a good idea? Why hadn't Rita stopped me? How'd I get this far without being caught?

Maybe, despite everything, I *was* lucky.

'Sorry,' I said. 'You live and you learn.'

Beth shook her head and smiled pure Hollywood.

'You're strange,' she said. She must have seen the effect that had on me. 'But good strange. I like strange. Anyway . . . I've got to get running. I'm never going to make the finish line otherwise. You know how long half a marathon is?'

'Five miles?' I said, thinking about everything but marathons.

'Thirteen. You want to run with me?'

I looked past her to the still pond.

'My groin's a bit tight,' I said. 'Sorry.'

CHAPTER
35

The Running Track of Life is Littered with Potholes

So my life of crime was officially over. I was both relieved and slightly disappointed but mostly in a panic about my unfinished History coursework.

Sitting in my bedroom, the longer the computer took to boot, the sorrier I felt. Life was like Windows. Constant waiting for something to happen, only to be disappointed when it finally did. I plugged a pair of earphones into the computer in the hope that their thick rubber would drown out the sound of the world outside my bedroom, not that there was any. It was one of those rare days when Mum and Dad were both at work. Rita was making like I didn't exist after I'd ruined her life by explaining the ATM hack hadn't worked.

I didn't access my coursework USB straight off. I

opened Chrome. I went to Facebook. Nothing. Someone had posted a video of own-goals from the Swedish second division and I watched it for twenty seconds. I went to Beth's page. She'd posted something, a picture from Instagram. She was smiling in her jogging kit and there was a link to her sponsorship page. I didn't click through. Fifty-three people had liked the image. Girls from school said she was a total babe. I scrolled through the likers' names. Many of the accompanying profile pictures were of people older than Mum and Dad. I got to Harry. His pic told you all you needed to know. Harry 101. He was balancing on a skateboard, like a dog on a ladder, at the top of a ramp. The image was taken from below and he was meant to look mean and moody. He didn't. The angle wasn't kind to his jawline and you could see up his nose. I went back to Beth's page and followed the link to her Insta account. There were a few extra snaps of a recent jog. The ice-cream pic. Harry had liked them all. So I went to his Insta page. The latest upload sent a machete shuddering through my skull. It was of two people sitting with their backs to the camera and looking out at a view, the type people post on Insta, some park, maybe Greenwich. I wasn't fussed by the aesthetic or the composition or the location. I didn't even question who'd taken the picture. Why? Because the figures were clearly Beth and Harry. And their shoulders, like I said, were close. Close close.

Close close close.

I tried zooming to see if they were holding hands. But, instead, I liked the picture, a little heart flashing red.

(Q: Could the day get any worse? A: Yes.)

I blamed the PC, the lag, my luck. I didn't even know I was signed in. Instantly I unliked. But the damage was done. I imagined Harry receiving an email alert. Laughing. Probably on his bed with a MacBook and spooning Beth and drinking expensive coffee out of golden mugs or whatever.

I stared into space until I decided there was nothing for it but homework. I was feeling miserable enough. Only idiots do schoolwork when they're happy. It's a waste of endorphins.

I opened my 'misery' Spotify playlist. I found the school USB and, after three attempts to insert the drive the correct way round, I stuck it in and waited for Windows to realise what was happening.

The drive was recognised and the first sign of another huge disaster, maybe the worst yet, was its name.

SanDisk.

And that was a problem because that was the name the drive was born with, before the user had a chance to edit it. The USB drive with my History coursework and also some English work and also a Java football game you could play undetected on the school computers was not named SanDisk. It was named 'Dylan Thomas is Great'. Of that (its name, I mean) I was sure and because I was sure I started to feel a creeping worry like an army of fat worms squirming through my intestines.

I opened SanDisk. It contained none of my schoolwork. What it did contain was a single file. Named 'ATMhack'.

My world collapsed. Remember when that volcano exploded in Iceland and it stopped flights for, like, three weeks? That's kind of what happened to my mind. Huge clouds of volcanic ash, lava flows, screaming Icelandic people.

In hindsight it had been a mistake to possess two identical USB drives, one for schoolwork and one for hacking banks' cash machines. Because the contents of this USB drive could mean only one thing:

Secreted in the external cash machine of a bank in Chislehurst was a USB drive not only named after me but also containing my coursework!!!

The implications of all this thumped testosterone

through my teenage frame. If someone found the USB, it wouldn't look good. Questions would be asked. By police officers. Was it a crime if there were no code? How much trouble could I get in for inserting my school USB into the cash machine? These were questions for Google.

I wasn't even sure I hadn't copied the code on to the school USB too. I'm idiot enough. Someone *would* find the drive. Tom had said. The engineers use the port to upgrade the software. The thing was a time bomb, waiting to explode me all the way to youth court.

And losing the drive meant I'd have to start my Vietnam essay again, which, in the short term, was more anxiety-inducing than the thought of jail.

I rose from the computer as the Hulk rises from Bruce Banner. Dumb luck made me a boy transformed. Here was my origin story.

I couldn't run the risk of incrimination by USB. I didn't have time to write those 1,500 words on the Vietnam War again.

Stopping only to check my phone (no alerts), I strode from my room, through to Rita's, smashing the door open with decisive palms. Rita was lying on her bed, headphones trailing from her netbook. She jumped at my entry and yanked her headphones from her ears, but before she could complain I spoke.

'It's on,' I said. 'Plan B.'

It turns out that I'd rob the bank after all.

This time, though, I'd be stealing back my History coursework instead of tens of thousands of pounds.

PART 3

CHAPTER 36

Operation RHC (Retrieve History Coursework)

The Window

- Problem 1: Its height.
- Solution 1: Climb on to one of the bins.
- Problem 2: Falling through the window on to the bank's hard floor.
- Solution 2: Take something soft to fall on to. A blanket?

The Alarm

- Problem 1: The alarm will sound.
- Solution 1: Break in on Saturday afternoon. People will think it's the same problem as last week – me trapped or another stray pigeon.

The Toilet Door

- Problem 1: It will probably be locked.
- Solution 1: I don't know. I've already been locked in there once and had to be freed by the fire brigade.

The Cash Machine

- Problem 1: It's locked with a keycode.
- Solution 1: *BOOBS*.
- Problem 2: It's also locked with a key.
- Solution 2: I don't know.

The Getaway

- Problem 1: Reaching up to the window.
- Solution 1: Hope they've mended the bin, which I broke. If they haven't, somehow use the sink and swing over?
- Problem 2: Leaving the bank.
- Solution 2: Get a lift with Rita.

CHAPTER 37

Fail to Prepare, Prepare to Fail

Early evening and I stood by my desk. The computer screen was tilted for Rita because, like a kindergarten kid, she was sitting cross-legged on the bedroom floor. Her focus was on the screen and specifically the PowerPoint. My PowerPoint. I'd spent the afternoon producing the thing, even turning down a kick-around, the first of the summer where the whole gang would be there, back from the holidays:

Ben Bright, who had a glass eye and would take it out for a pound; Chris 'Rose' Rosemary, who could mis-control the ball further than most could pass it; Si Warhurst and his sister, Emma, who was fifty times better than Si and got on BBC Kent when she wasn't picked for the first XI; Dan Hirst, who had all the skills but would have been beaten in a sprint by my gran; Carlton Smith, who'd punch you if you tackled him; the Walker twins, one girl and one boy, both as equally crap as the other; and James Woods, who was so serious about playing in goal that he owned 'professional standard' gloves, even though they never stopped him conceding ten in every match.

Yes, I'd turned them all down. For a PowerPoint presentation. Desperate times call for desperate measures.

I'd drawn the curtains to create the right atmos. Telling Rita there'd be an opportunity for questions at the end, I moved through slides with a tap of the space-bar.

My plan was simple: gain access to the bank by climbing through the bar-less toilet window, break through the toilet door to the bank's rear corridor and (somehow) unlock the ATM access panel to retrieve my USB.

'So I've got some questions,' said Rita when I'd finished. I nodded permission. 'Two of your problems don't have solutions. And they're both to do with locks, which seems kind of key, pun intended.'

'That's not a question,' I said, remembering the days of the lower-school lecture competition.

'I've not finished. Also – I'm not picking you up because you might be happy to get arrested but I'm not. I didn't get the grades to go to Manchester to become a getaway driver. Especially when there's no cash on offer.'

'That wasn't a question either.'

Rita shrugged.

I didn't want to argue. Not now. This was my bedroom; the lack of light and stink of deodorant proved as much. It was my plan too. That meant *I* was in charge. And we were here to discuss strategy. Not to fight.

'I don't want to get arrested either, Rita. That's why I did the PowerPoint. Do you actually have any questions or are we done?'

'Here's a question – are you going to use the correct USB this time? Are you actually going to get some money?'

If the devil had a form, its form would be Rita, my big sister. I noticed she didn't say 'steal'.

'What do you think?' I asked, knowing exactly what she thought.

'The plan, because you burnt down your friend's house—'

'It was faulty wiring . . .'

'Whatever. The plan was to use this hack code to steal

231

sixty thousand pounds. And it was perfect because you'd never get caught. The code deletes itself, am I right? You said it even disabled the ATM's camera. Like an invisibility cloak.'

'You *really* want a MacBook, don't you?'

Rita shrugged and we stared like dogs sizing each other up before the inevitable bum sniff. But I wasn't getting my backside smelt. That's gross. *And* I'd designed a PowerPoint, so I deserved respect.

'No,' I said. 'I'm not robbing the bank. That's crazy. I don't even know what I was thinking. I just need to get my coursework back. It's got my name on it and everything.'

Rita stared.

Rita shrugged.

'Maybe you're right,' she said eventually. 'You can't leave the house without tripping over, so how you'd manage to rob a bank, I don't know.'

'So are you going to help?' Rita pulled out her phone. 'What are you doing?'

'Helping you. Googling how to break locks.'

'Don't!' I said, an impotent hand rushing out.

'Chill, fam,' she said. 'It's interesting. Imagine the fun at uni if I could pick locks. And, anyway, I'm on private browsing.'

'That doesn't make any difference.'

'Well, if you get caught, you can say you stole my phone too. What type of lock is it?'

CHAPTER 38

Don't Forget the Importance of Good Timing

On my duvet:

1. Three screwdrivers of different sizes, borrowed from Dad's toolbox

2. A pair of adjustable pliers, also borrowed from Dad's toolbox

3. My spare pillow, the fat marshmallow one that'd break your neck if you tried sleeping on it

4. The rucksack that Mum bought off eBay for the adventure course I'd meant to do at Easter, pulled from the cupboard under the stairs where everything goes but nothing returns

5. A (used) Amazon gift voucher, rectangular and plastic like a credit card

6. A Casio watch Rita had found in her drawers

7. A pink ski mask with a few strands of blonde hair stuck to it. (In *Heat*, Robert De Niro uses one, although it's not pink. There were no cameras round the back of the bank, none in the rear corridor either, but it pays to play it extra safe.)

8. Latex gloves that came with Rita's hair dye and looked very serial killer

The days between the PowerPoint presentation and *the* Saturday were spent in cryogenic suspension like when astronauts travel to distant galaxies. Only my brain hadn't been frozen because the part that worried remained functional. And then some.

Normally it takes ages for the weekend to come, especially during termtime. But not now, not this week. At least the speed with which the days flew past left me less opportunity to worry about Tuesday's new academic year, especially since I'd done no work.

I had *tried*. Reading three books off the list our English teacher had handed out. But I couldn't concentrate. Not because I wasn't enjoying them, not because of the constant temptation of my phone or *Football Manager*, but because life was currently more dramatic than fiction.

I also picked my nails and checked my bank balance (I still hadn't been paid) and lay on my bed and messaged Beth about how I couldn't come jogging because my groin strain was still problematic. It was best to avoid her until the weekend. I didn't want to be talked out of anything. She was probably off with Harry somewhere too. And as much as confessing had felt good at the time, there were still things that were better she didn't know. Things that made me look like an idiot. Like the plan to break into a bank to retrieve the USB with my History coursework on it, for instance.

My real fear, as I stared at the cracked plaster of my ceiling, imagining the spiderweb fractures to be strange coastlines, was that Gradual had replaced the window bars. Because he'd have to sort them out sometime soon. I mean, the window was a weak point. That was central to my plan. But they'd still been absent at the start of the week, the window a toothless smile, when I'd cycled by to check, so . . .

I got ready. I showered. I ate a sensible breakfast: two Weetabix, no sugar. Rita suggested a black coffee, but I knew I couldn't trust my bladder. And when I was ready to leave, having studied the PowerPoint a couple more times, she placed her hands on the straps of my mostly-empty-but-supposedly-hungry-for-money rucksack. She stared into my eyes and asked if I'd remembered the right USB stick with the hack code.

I nodded and she wished me luck. She leant in and kissed my forehead. When she stepped back, she looked like she was about to say something. But she didn't, so I grunted and turned away because every crime starts with a single step. Also, Rita was making the moment hyper-real and stressing me out.

I left the house to Mum shouting that I should pick up a pint of milk if I had the chance. I walked into the dying suburban summer feeling convinced my attempt to rob a local bank by crawling through a toilet window couldn't end in success. Stepping over Kevin's gravestone, fortune and glory had never felt so distant.

And it was school next week.

Rita and me had agreed the following timing:

Thirteen-thirty, I leave the house, under the pretence of going to play football. I'd arrive at the bank at 14.00, according to Google Maps, and would then proceed with the robbery, leaving at 14.10. If police responded to the alarm, which they'd never done so far, I'd calculated it would take thirteen minutes to scramble from Bromley Police Station, unless I was particularly unlucky and a squad car happened to be passing. That gave me a window of three minutes to get clear, worst-case scenario. At 14.11, Mum and Dad and Rita would be waiting outside, stuffed into Mum's Ford Fiesta, ready to collect me from 'football practice' and drive to lunch in Blackheath to celebrate Rita's A-level results . . . at Rita's suggestion . . . because why not?

I walked and I checked my phone. No new alerts. It was my nerves, electric like Dr Doom, that forced my idiot fingers to open Beth's Instagram. The latest picture: a shot of Harry on his skateboard. On the Southbank. All soft filters and implied closeness. I quickened my pace. She shouldn't be taking pictures of Harry. I deleted the app. For the third time this summer, I turned the phone off and dropped it into the rucksack.

The route from my house to the bank was straightforward. Literally. I just needed to keep walking. Whatever day of the week, whatever time of day, this road was heavy with cars. But not today. There'd not even been the usual sprinkling of weekend cyclists with their Lycra beer bellies and midlife crises.

Maybe everyone had gone to Dreamland? Or Diggerland? Or Teapot Island?

But the longer I walked, the more the emptiness

creeped me out. Was this the zombie apocalypse? Or was I still dreaming? Not one car. Not even a bus. Was I being watched? Was I being filmed? Was I the star of a hit reality TV show and didn't know it?

And then came the drumming.

Initially I took it to be my heartbeat. As the tarmac beneath my feet began to shake I realised that the sound was actually made up of many components. A drumming, a rolling of thunder, getting . . . closer.

You know when it's just about to chuck it down? One fat raindrop explodes on the ground, the storm's vanguard, then comes another, and soon there's hundreds of the bad boys splashing all around you and before you know it you're running for shelter because it's bucketing down?

That's what it was like for me walking on the narrow pavement of the road that cuts through Chislehurst woods and out on to the high street, only it wasn't raining rain. It was raining joggers. And they weren't falling from the sky. They were huffing and puffing down the middle of the road.

Before I knew it I was overwhelmed by Lycra. Runners, travelling up the empty road like Coca-Cola from the mouth of a shaken bottle. Some looked at Fitbits. Some looked like they were about to collapse. And weirdly they passed with a smell exactly like Rita's deodorant.

Each jogger wore a piece of paper pinned to their back. The paper showed a number and above the number the words: CHISLEHURST HALF-MARATHON.

CHAPTER 39

Never Underestimate your own Potential for Stupidity

I'm an idiot, I thought, *a massive idiot, just like Beth said. The Galactic Emperor of All Idiots, sent to Earth to show humanity true idiocy.*

Saturday. The day of Beth's half-marathon. The one I *knew* she'd been training for. And the worst time to commit a crime ever because the streets were awash with witnesses. I thought of all the friends and family who'd soon be reading of the race on social media.

I pulled out my phone. The first rush of runners had gone. Now groups ebbed and flowed past. All had red faces. All stumbled forward as if every step was as doubly painful as the last.

Where was Beth? Had she passed? Or was she

approaching? Had she seen me already? I turned. Dotted faces, all ages, colours, genders. United in agony. But no Beth.

I started walking at a good pace. Forward. Because turning round would make Beth more likely to appear and I'd not even sponsored her.

I tapped out a WhatsApp to Rita. My fingers trembled.

Abort, abort, I wrote.

Rita is typing . . .

? came the eventual reply.

Marathon. People everywhere.

Such was the seriousness of the moment, I avoided emoji.

Rita is typing . . .

Police tied up. Roads closed = even better, she replied, adding the okay hand.

Up ahead, an elderly man in a straw hat was sitting in a deckchair in the middle of the road. He was holding up a laminated A4 piece of paper, printed with a thick arrow that directed runners to take the dogleg turn-off away from the common and the pond and the ducks and the high street and the bank.

Hmm, I thought, smiling at the man as I did.

The high street was deserted. Further up, a purple

tape stretched across the road, tied between two lamp-posts. This must be the finish because I could see a woman unpacking mineral water from a case and a man looking at a clipboard. Both of them wore high-vis jackets and had exactly the faces people who help organise local half-marathons have.

I figured that the race must loop back and round to finish a hundred metres further along from the bank. This stretch of the high street, therefore, about the size of three tennis courts, was cut out from the route – dead space between the old guy with the laminated arrow and the finishing line. It'd be full of bent-double runners soon enough, when the race was run, but right then there was nothing but a crushed cardboard coffee cup. It was almost as if the area had been cleared for me, a launch pad or a stage.

Question: where would Mum and Dad pick me up if the road were closed?

I WhatsApped Rita again. Sometimes it's good to have a sister.

Change of plan. Pick up Sains car park. Five mins later than plan. Probs leave home early too.

Sure, came the reply.

Sainsbury's would never be closed, even if this did turn

243

out to be the zombie apocalypse and not the Chislehurst half-marathon.

I ran round the back of the bank and there was nothing but me and the bins (and their rotten vegetables) and the toilet window, *still without bars*. I pulled a black bin under the window, a bin exactly like the one Dad gets me to carry out front every Thursday morning. And I yanked on Rita's pink ski mask and the tight fabric made me feel withdrawn, like a tiny voice rattling around somebody else's body. I found the latex gloves in the bottom of the bag. They took forever to put on but eventually I managed it – I wasn't going to leave any fingerprints behind.

I climbed on to the bin and it wobbled, but I caught my balance, steadying myself against the bank's brick. The window was narrower than I remembered, but the bin had positioned me at a perfect height for breaking and entering. The glass shone proudly and was level with my chest. And so I pulled the pliers from the rucksack. It was a bit awkward and I almost fell off the bin.

Time check: 14.00 on the nose. Gulp. I checked over my shoulder. Tarmac leading to tall trees. No eyes. No cameras. No Rita. No police. No joggers. No dogs. No Beth.

Only the past.

And ahead stretched the future and also a tiny window to break through.

I pulled back the pliers.

Let's get lucky, I thought.

No! hissed every synapse in my brain.

As I swung the pliers I closed my eyes.

(This History coursework had better get full marks.)

CHAPTER 40

Don't Try to Rob a Bank on Your Own

The glass smashed like glass does when you whack it with a bit of metal. And as it smashed a faint cheer erupted from the high street. The race was finishing and somebody had probably managed their personal best.

The bank's alarm didn't go off. Not immediately. No neighbours, and no police, came running. Because glass gets broken all the time. It's south-east London. No, the alarm only began its whoop-whoop-whooping when I shoved my bedroom pillow through the broken window, its fat white fabric knocking out most of the *T. rex*-tooth glass that'd survived. One tall shard, a skyscraper in a skyline of bungalows, managed to endure even the pillow, but stood no chance with what came next, my rucksack, which I pushed through like a tiny postman working at a massive letter box. Already the alarm had penetrated the reptilian centre of my brain. My ears pulsed like there'd never been anything but the alarm and the alarm was everything.

I reached through the window space, unhitched its arm, and pulled open the frame. With the bin wobbling underfoot and the silver rectangle heavy on the back of my head, I pulled myself into the bank. The frame scraped down my neck and along my spine. There was something fishlike about my entry, a limbless movement through dead space.

The forward motion stalled when I was half in and half out, the windowsill and bar stumps sharp against my stomach, with my legs outside and my everything else inside. If a passer-by had seen the window, they'd have thought they were in east London and I was performance art.

Looking down at the toilet floor the pillow and rucksack called to me. *As long as I protect my head*, I thought, *I'll be all right.*

(How'd I ever think a single pillow could catch my whole body?)

'You're an idiot, Dylan,' I mouthed, starting to believe I really was.

It would be a soft landing. But not an easy landing.

I wriggled forward, like a worm, readying myself to plummet. A centimetre further inside and my weight tipped the gravitational seesaw and I fell, Converse knocking against the window frame as they passed through.

I fell. But not to the floor.

The cuff of my right trouser leg caught. My descent stopped with my nose a sniff away from the pillow. I swept the padding out of the way with a suspended, upside-down arm and then was stuck for a bit doing a strange handstand, just hanging as if someone had paused this part. But, with the sound of fabric ripping, something that'd annoy Mum more than any bank robbing, my leg broke free, and I crumpled on to the floor. Dangling by your trouser leg seemed to be a family skill.

I was in.

I collected the rucksack and pulled out the Amazon gift card. As I rushed to the door handle, I spotted a new rubbish bin, meaning I had something to clamber on to when making my escape. With rucksack on back and card in hand, I knelt at the door in a position suitable for a locksmith: phase two of the master plan.

I'd learnt to use a card from Rita's YouTube search. In the video, a man, whose profile pic was a frog, spoke

248

in an accent from the Deep South and, holding a doorknob identical to the one in the bank's toilet, demonstrated what you needed to do if you'd forgotten your key. The trick was to wedge your credit card in the gap where the lock's bolt crosses from door to frame, apply a bit of pressure, and *voilà!*

'It might bend your card a piddlin',' he'd said.

The video had the warning THIS IS FOR EDUCATIONAL PORPOISES ONLY and I'd watched it more times in the last week than I had the compilation of Palace's best ever goals in my whole life.

My right hand shook with tiny tremors as I gripped the handle. If not for the continuing klaxon, I'd have heard the metal jangle. My left hand, unfamiliar with precision but called upon in this hour of need due to the doorknob/door-frame dynamic, wedged the plastic card between lock and frame. I summoned up the memory of the video, and forced the plastic downwards. It needed proper muscle to move, but move it did and with a satisfying click I felt through the doorknob.

I stood, pulling open the door. The Amazon gift card, bent at forty-five degrees along the middle, fell to the floor.

It actually worked, I thought.

I picked up the card and continued.

(What other secrets could you learn through YouTube?)

Up ahead: the corridor. Could I smell coffee? Could I taste the air conditioning? Or was adrenalin muddling my mind?

I'll tell you what I couldn't do – and that's see. In my PowerPoint I'd not considered the problem of light. It was the afternoon: I'd assumed there'd be loads of the stuff. But the back corridor was windowless, a thin artery running between the cashiers' desks and the back rooms. There'd be a light switch somewhere, but I couldn't waste time looking for it, so, as I stepped forward, the only light accompanying me was the really-not-up-for-it illumination from the toilet. This darkness made the crime seem proper shady. I swept the rucksack from my back and found my phone. I'd powered it down because I didn't want mobile towers triangulating a record of me being here. But I needed its light. I turned it on and switched quickly to airplane mode. Twelve minutes until Mum and Dad were due in the supermarket car park. Time to get moving. I turned and tripped over my rucksack. And because I was holding my phone in one hand and the tangled straps in the other, my latex hands

250

weren't quick enough to protect my face. My ski-masked chin skidded across the bare carpet like wood against sandpaper. I was quick to my feet, unlike a Premier League striker, because this was no time to be rolling around in darkened corridors.

I pulled up the fabric from my jawline. My chin stung, I'd broken the gravestone scab, but the iPhone's light didn't pick up any blood on the gloves or carpet. I wanted to leave as little DNA evidence as possible.

The ATM access panel: let's do this thing.

CHAPTER 41

Robbing a Bank is a Matter of Holding Your Nerve

A deep breath because that's what TV/film bank robbers do before committing themselves to their safes.

'Boobs,' I said but couldn't hear the word because of the alarm, which pulsed a wave of pain across the front of my head as it continued to highlight my presence to a world that, so far, didn't care.

Bad luck, alarm.

How about another breath?

Clint Eastwood.

Al Pacino.

George Clooney.

And another?

I fingered the keypad.

8.0.0.8.5.

BOOBS.

The LED light at the top right of the black plastic border blinked from red to green. I grinned a Tom grin because there were tons of variables this afternoon but he and his boobs had been there for me. They would never have let me down. Not in a million years. How'd I ever doubted that 80085 would be the code?

And now for the final lock, the last step before the insides of the ATM were revealed. YouTube had found an American, a girl with freckles and pigtails, shoving a small screwdriver into the lock of a school locker, the type you see in every American film with high-school kids ever. She squeezed its grip with a pair of adjustable pliers and smashed down on the silver legs of the pliers with her elbow. She fell to the floor and whoever was filming the whole thing laughed. But the lock was broken and the locker swung open. They stuffed a fish head behind a stack of textbooks and they both found it very funny and the word PUNKED flashed across the picture.

It didn't look too difficult.

I laid my phone on the floor and its light cast my face in Halloween shadows. From the rucksack I pulled the first screwdriver my fingers found. Its blade was too thick for the lock. I found the second screwdriver. This blade was smaller, but still too thick and too wide to fit. I licked my lips. I wiped imaginary sweat from my forehead and scratched at my chin. Let's find the third screwdriver. Because it wouldn't fail me. I had faith in it. It was still in the rucksack. Its size had yet to be decided. All I needed to do was believe it would fit.

I repeated the mantra – *Clint Eastwood, Al Pacino, George Clooney . . . Ron Livingston.* Repeat, repeat, repeat. Repetition makes confidence.

I pulled out the final screwdriver. And it slid deep into the lock as if created only for this purpose, as if its whole life, like mine, had been leading up to this moment.

Find the adjustable pliers. Grab the screwdriver's grip with their eager jaws. Tighten the pliers until they lock the screwdriver in a death-bite. Check they're connected and steady. Think of the girl in the YouTube video. She used her forearm, like a wrestler's neck crush. Steady and . . . action!

Wait! Was that a sound? I freeze. Did I hear something? Had there been a bang? A something? A pigeon or the police? Should I run to the toilet to check?

Focus. There's nothing but the alarm. Yes, focus. No, there's

nothing but the cash machine. Best get back to it. No time to waste.

I slammed my arm against the pliers. They turned with a jolt from ninety to one hundred and eighty degrees. Life lesson: brute force rules. I pulled out the screwdriver and gripped at the cash machine's back door. It opened without protest and there, in all the beauty of plastic and metal and wires was my USB drive. I pulled it out and dropped it in the rucksack. Job done.

But I didn't close up straight away. Because it still wasn't fair we had no money. And, even though time continued ticking and my heart continued racing, I paused. I sat there at the open cash machine, pondering.

The cash-machine cartridges were assembled in two rows of three across the bottom of the square of electronics. Full of banknotes. I could meet Beth at the finish, I could hand over an envelope full of money, I could shower her with twenty-pound notes as she crossed the line. It would be stupid and I'd be immediately arrested, but still . . .

'Up to you,' I'd say. 'Sponsorship money or deposit for your flat.'

I'd say I'd won the lottery.

My thinking was broken by a voice. And the voice

shouted over the alarm. And the voice came from the other side of the cash machine. The outside world and adults and the half-marathon and punishment.

'Bruv!' it shouted. 'Are you inside the machine? Are you working it? No, I'm joking. But I can hear you banging about. You must be tiny, mate.' I couldn't see any figure. The ATM protected me. But, outside, a man *was* shouting. And claiming he could hear me. Could he? Maybe he was drunk? People talk to all kinds of things. Dad talks to his van, I mean . . . Could the outside man see me? Not likely. Only the screen was exposed and there was no way of him being able to see through that. I hesitated. I listened. Another softer voice murmured about alarms. When it stopped the shouter continued. 'Are you robbing this, then? You in there?' he called. 'Fair play. But leave us a fifty for the weekend.'

A chill passed through my body like the future me was thinking about this moment in a tiny prison cell with all the regret in the world.

I looked at the money. And what came to mind was the ending of *Indiana Jones and the Last Crusade.*

CHAPTER
42

Take Inspiration from Everywhere and Everything

Indiana Jones and the Last Crusade – a great chasm has opened in the ground, down which the Holy Grail, something the Nazis have spent the film trying to get their hands on, has fallen, coming to rest on a shelf of rock. A Nazi woman has tripped into the hole too. Indiana Jones has managed to grab one wrist but can't pull her up without her other arm. Unfortunately she's using that to try to reach the Grail.

'Honey, I can't hold you,' he says.

Her black glove slips from Indy's grasp and the Nazi woman falls into the smoky abyss, screaming. Overbalanced, Indiana Jones follows her, only to be caught by his father. Henry Jones Sr, as before, has only managed to grasp one arm. Indy stretches for the Holy Grail, his fingertips making contact.

'Indiana,' says his dad (Sean Connery). 'Let it go.'

(And a million years before *Frozen*.)

Indy lets it go.

I didn't need thousands of pounds. Well, I did. And Beth did too. But this wasn't the way to get it. You know that weird lightening of your thoughts when you're making a hard choice but one you know is right? Like fessing up to copying and pasting an English essay off the web? Yeah, that feeling.

(Anyway, I should at least wait for my GCSE results before committing to a life of crime.)

Letting it go, I closed up the ATM, somehow managing to flick the lock back to working order. I secured the access panel over it. It was as if I'd never been there. LOL.

'Oi,' shouted the voice on the other side but it was best to ignore all this until I'd managed to escape, I decided.

The time was 1408. Eight minutes until Mum and Dad. I rushed for the pool of light waiting at the toilet door, beckoning me from the darkness. And there was the window looking smaller than ever. I moved the bin underneath it, and I swear the alarm became louder and more insistent than ever, like it knew I was getting away and wasn't happy about it. I took a hand to the sink to steady myself as I turned the bin over and stepped up. It must have been bought from Poundland because as soon as I stepped on to its upturned plastic, it collapsed. It would have been better to stand on a paper cup.

Could I do this without the bin? The window was high but I could get my hands to it. So I half pulled myself up, easy, but my Converse with their worn tread skidded frantically across the wall. My muscles burnt and with the inevitability of gravity I fell, striking the floor with a thump that'd make you purse your lips and suck the air. But my head hit the pillow, so at least I hadn't been knocked out because that would have been proper bad.

I took a deep breath. *Think.*

The pillow needed to go before me. As did the rucksack. Even if I managed to pull myself up, I'd never squeeze through the space with a bag on my back.

This was good thinking.

Standing on tiptoes, I shoved the pillow through. It disappeared into the outside, into freedom, the sunshine and chain restaurants, the glorious emptiness that called to me and stretched out in every direction around the bank.

I paused before pushing the rucksack through. Because what if someone was on the other side? What if a passing dog saw? But I had no choice. I couldn't get through wearing the bag.

I took a running jump, thinking I could propel myself airwards enough to get a good hold of the window ledge. All I needed to do was get my elbows up there and I'd be able to pull through. *Muscles, don't fail me now.*

(Why hadn't I taken PE more seriously? If I'd spent time at the gym, like the Walker twins, I'd have plenty of upper-body strength. No problem. *And* I'd be popular because of my buff torso.)

So I ran and I jumped and my fingertips, wet and hot in their latex gloves, missed completely, clawing not at freedom but at dead wall. I could feel the heat under my armpits, my breathing was everywhere, and my heart wasn't beating – it was breakdancing. Were those tears? Or were my eyes sweating?

I mounted the sink. Its enamel pulled cracks from the wall, but it held. With my right foot at the taps I pushed my palms against the wall in an attempt to Spider-Man it across. And I almost did. The little finger of my left hand touched the nearest corner recess of the window. And then I overbalanced and I fell and this time there was no pillow to catch me. The left side of my body slapped against the unforgiving lino. I didn't feel pain. Only a frustration on the edge of transforming into complete, paralytic panic. Because almost isn't good enough. Shots that *almost* go in aren't goals.

Once again, I pulled myself up to stand. I'd spent much of the afternoon pulling myself up. The suits in *Reservoir Dogs* don't trip. You only fall over in *GTA* if a car hits you.

Here's the moment of victory, I thought. *PMA*, I thought. Heroes always face adversity. It's not a bomb. It's a window. And it's not even that high. I've climbed taller trees. Back when I climbed trees.

I stepped to it. I gripped the ledge. I focused my complete willpower, all my Weetabix energy, to my fingers, arms and shoulders. I pulled and I pulled. My feet rose from the floor, and my shoes squeaked against the wall looking for purchase as I continued pulling, a huge arc of burning pain running from left hand to right hand. But I wasn't getting any higher and I let go and I dropped to my feet and felt a wave of anxiety body-slam me. What if I never escaped? Trapped at the scene of my own crime,

I'd succeeded in retrieving the USB stick but I'd failed in that other key component – getting out.

Good work, Dylan. You've excelled yourself this time.

A scream sounded. But it wasn't me. It was Rita. Her face suddenly stared down from the window, mostly covered by a bandana tied across her mouth like she was in a Mexican drug cartel. Lovely Rita. Saints must feel what I felt when they see Jesus's face and all that. An overwhelming gratefulness, an all-embracing love, a bladder sting. The fabric of her face mask, a black-and-white peacock design, shivered and she shouted really loudly:

'Come on, you melt!'

Either side of her face, hands appeared and snaked into the room and beckoned me forward. I ran, and leapt, gripping those bad boys and clinging on like they were the last lifeboat on the *Titanic*. I never thought skinny Rita, my weakling sister, would ever be capable of lifting me. Literally or otherwise. Maybe all that texting meant she had over-developed arm tendons? She gripped my hands with steel-cable strength and pulled back from her side of the window. Either her force was going to pull my arms from their sockets or she was going to free me from the toilety prison.

Finally my Converse found traction and, with my

shoulders singing hallelujahs, I managed to get enough of my arms up and out of the toilet window to pull the rest of my body with them. Rita, outside on the rubbish bin, the sturdy one, hooked her arms under my shoulders and helped ease me out until I was able to pivot a leg and slide free of the window in a weird, crunched foetal position.

My limbs were all over the shop. Down I went and smashed into the bin like a pinball hits the bumper. This sent Rita tumbling and we fell to the ground in a heap of brother and sister.

'Your chin is bleeding through your ski mask,' she shouted as she got up. 'Gross.'

She grabbed the pillow as I found the rucksack, sliding it on to my back like a hiking pro. I pulled off my mask as Rita removed her bandana. The fabric pricked my chin as it ripped away.

And the bank alarm continued its wah-wah-wah.

Rita made to run round the nearside of the bank, a route that would have taken us directly to the person who thought there was someone hiding in the cash machine. I grabbed her arm and led her the other way. It meant jumping over a metre-high wall (for dwarves or terriers?) into the pay-and-display car park, but she

263

followed without moaning or, at least, the alarm drowned out any complaint.

I suddenly realised I really needed a wee.

A few steps into the car park and we stopped. Rita was still holding the pillow. Around us, south-east London stirred with runners. With our heavy breathing and our hearts thumping, we might have just finished the run ourselves. The afternoon sun cast heavy shadows on the tarmac. My chin hurt.

'Did you?' she asked.

'No,' I said.

'Good.'

If looks could kill, my glare would have knocked her down.

'Right,' I said and asked if Mum and Dad were in Sainsbury's car park.

'Yeah, but Dad's popped in to get doughnuts. I couldn't stop him.'

CHAPTER 43

There's Nothing More Important
Than Your Getaway Plan

There was no longer a ribbon across the road. Those runners crossing the finishing line were looking more like grandparents than elite athletes and the pavements were emptying of friends and family. If it hadn't been for the rubbish bins overflowing with plastic water bottles, and the lack of cars, you might not have guessed there was anything unusual to the day. Okay, the alarm continued but nobody important seemed bothered. There were no police, no sirens. We passed a community support officer, a fake cop, and she was wandering towards the bank in no hurry and she was even whistling.

I'd looked back at the cash machine. There was nobody at it. The guy who'd been speaking to me had obviously managed to withdraw his fifty pounds. He'd rationalised the weird noises behind the ATM in the same way we all do when something out of the ordinary happens. I saw a ghost when I was four. But I reckon it was proof that eating cheese before bedtime messes with your mind, instead of evidence of the afterlife.

Rita led the way, weaving in and out of pedestrians. Up ahead was the beautiful orange of Sainsbury's. *So*, I thought, my breath returning to normal, *this was it*. I had Sunday and Monday to finish off the History and then it'd be the new school year, the cycle beginning again as if nothing had happened.

Next holiday I'd try to keep it quiet.

And then Rita stopped. I was about to ask why when a woman, all smiles, held open her arms and said, 'Dylan Thomas!' It was Beth's mum. 'Long time no see. Writing any poetry yet?'

Anybody else and I'd have made my excuses and continued walking.

'Not yet,' I said. 'Hello, Mrs Fraser.'

'Is this your sister?' she asked.

I didn't reply. Because Mrs Fraser wasn't alone. There was also Mr Fraser. And . . . Beth, standing in her purple marathon kit, eating a banana and smiling as best she could with a mouth full of banana and looking as if sunlight shone from her skin.

'Hi, Beth,' I said. 'Well done.'

She swallowed.

'I'm just eating a banana,' she said and leant in for a hug. And even though she was wet with sweat and smelt of banana I didn't care.

'What happened to your chin?' asked Mrs Fraser.

'I tripped over a gravestone.'

'Ouch. Nobody you knew, I hope.'

Mr Fraser said hello. He also said how nice it was for Beth's friends to show support. He was acting less angry than usual. More smiley.

'Why've you got a pillow? In case you get bored?' he asked Rita, elbowing his wife in the ribs and laughing and pointing.

Rita smiled, cuddling the pillow to her chest as if it were a teddy bear.

'How long have you been here?' asked Beth. 'Hi, Rita! Where were you standing?'

'Umm,' I said. 'Around here.'

'Hi,' said Rita.

'We didn't see you,' said Mrs Fraser.

And there, in the distance, a siren. I could definitely hear it. Rita could too, because—

'Our parents are waiting,' she said, stepping away from Beth's family, so they couldn't see when she raised her eyebrows and mouthed a swearword and frantically pointed to Sainsbury's.

'How'd you rip your trousers, Dylan?' asked Beth's mum. 'I'd get that sewn up before your mother sees it. Kids!'

The adults chuckled.

'Our parents,' said Rita.

'We're all going for a pizza if you two want to come along and freeload,' said Beth's dad. 'We've a lot to celebrate. My treat.'

'It's just . . .' said Rita, edging further away.

I was about to make up an excuse, like I'd been doing all summer, but an electric light bulb of a bright idea struck me.

'Are you sure?' I asked. 'Whereabouts?'

(Here it is: an alibi! And a gold-plated one too. 'No, officer, I couldn't have broken into the bank. I was watching the marathon and eating pizza. Anyway, you'll find that nothing was stolen. Not that I know.')

'Blackheath Pizza Express,' said Beth, rolling her eyes. 'And I'm sooo sweaty and gross.'

'Dylan . . .' said Rita, the siren now almost as loud as the bank alarm.

'You're not gross,' I said.

'Watch it,' said Beth's dad.

Blackheath is a good ten minutes' drive from Chislehurst. I slipped the rucksack from my shoulders because maybe bumping into the Frasers wasn't all bad.

'Could you take this to the car?' I said, handing Rita the bag.

Her eyes looked like they might fall from her head.

'Alibi,' I mouthed and I don't think anyone else saw.

'You're welcome too,' said Beth's dad to Rita. 'The more the merrier.'

Either she understood me or she'd lost her patience.

'I'm lactose intolerant,' she said. 'Thanks anyway.'

She offered a quick wave and broke into a jog towards Sainsbury's.

'Rita!' I called.

She looked over her shoulder.

'Thanks.'

And she smiled.

Don't Forget to Eat

Mum and Dad would be angry I was missing Rita's celebratory lunch but I'm sure they'd get over it, not least because Rita had only suggested it as a cover for my bank raid. It made good criminal sense to split from her. And using Beth's family as getaway drivers was a bonus.

Especially as a siren was now almost upon us. We turned to watch a passing ambulance steer round the last few finishing joggers then off and away, its noise fading as it went.

'Someone's collapsed, then,' said Beth's dad as if it were funny.

We drove to the restaurant in the Frasers' Ford Fiesta. Rita rolled her eyes as her dad spoke without pause about how running a marathon was like preparing for exams.

The longer he spoke, the angrier he sounded. I stopped listening around the time I saw a motorbike driven by a rider in an Iron Man mask. Shortly after it had passed, and as we waited in the inevitable south London traffic, I swear the bank's alarm stopped.

(In the back of the car I did a subtle, hidden fist pump. Not even Beth saw. Tiny fireworks of the mind exploded, spelling out the word SUCCESS. Because I'd done it. And I'd not got caught. And I was about to eat free pizza.)

I looked to Beth. I smiled. As Mr Fraser loudly described how you should revise like you were training for a marathon I wondered if he'd treat us to dessert too.

In the restaurant he ordered Prosecco. I thought maybe this bigging-up of Beth's successful run was a bit much, I mean it was only a *half*-marathon, but it turned out this wasn't the only thing the family were celebrating.

Get this: Beth explained that the social media coverage of the burning miniature White House had caught the attention of no less than the (American) owner of Crystal Palace Football Club.

Mr Fraser smiled. 'Diamond geezer,' he said.

He'd commissioned Beth's dad to build him a new White House in Beckenham. Not only that, he'd transferred enough money up front on the very day of the deadline so that the Fraser family were able to pay for their new apartment.

'You couldn't make it up,' said Mr Fraser. 'I'm almost happy our family home burnt down in the first place.'

'Not that we're going to be in the flat permanently,' said Mrs Fraser.

'I don't know . . .' said her husband.

His voice trailed off as Mrs Fraser stared angrily at him.

'Why are you wearing so much black?' Beth asked me.

'I don't know,' I said. 'I'm emo?'

She didn't look convinced. She looked like she was thinking. I ordered an American Hot and Mrs Fraser said I was a joker, what with the White House having burnt down.

Halfway through the meal, with the adults occupied by talk about insurance rates, I dared ask about Harry.

'He's gross,' she said. I tried not to smile. 'He tried to kiss me in an underpass. *So* not cool.'

I didn't say I'd seen his Insta pictures. I didn't say anything. Apart from 'gross' because, straight up, I couldn't think of anything worse than Harry trying to kiss you. Especially in an underpass.

'How's your groin?' asked Beth, kind of changing the subject.

'Getting better,' I said, looking at my pizza to avoid her lie-detector eyes.

When it came time to pay I pretended to fiddle with my wallet. Beth put her hand on my hand and said her dad had it covered.

'Rolling in cash now,' he said.

Mrs Fraser told him not to be so vulgar and, turning to me, asked what my plans for the afternoon were.

'Actually, Mum, me and Dylan were planning on doing something together,' said Beth, kicking me under the table.

'No chance,' said Mrs Fraser. 'You've got unpacking to do. And showering too.'

Beth explained they'd packed up what they'd taken to the high-rise apartment in the expectation of moving out. Now the American money meant they could stay, there was unpacking to do.

(Was she expecting me to offer to help?)

'What about meeting on Monday?' I said. 'The last day of the holidays.'

'It's a date,' said Beth.

'Watch yourselves,' growled her dad.

CHAPTER 45

The End

On Monday we met in Chislehurst.

'Your chin's looking better,' she said as she grabbed my hand.

Don't think for one moment that this was a romantic moment of physical contact, the one thing every fifteen-year-old in the world wants, apart from a new console and his team to win the league. Because it wasn't. She was half a step ahead and leading me forward like a mother pulling a toddler with a full nappy to the nearest toilet.

'Where are we going?' I asked.

'Who knows?'

I told her there was something I had to do before all that.

We turned off the pavement and up to the bank, a place I'd be totally chill with never visiting ever again in my whole life. The place, I'm pleased to say, had its security shutters down and was proper closed, because it was bank holiday Monday.

She laughed. 'You're not going to break in?'

She was wearing dungarees and Doc Martens. Despite this I felt a growing warmth, like when you've eaten too much pizza, like when Rita rescued me from the toilet window. But, if I'm honest, more intensely.

'No,' I said, getting my debit card from my wallet and sliding it into the ATM. I entered my PIN and tried for fifty quid. The machine hesitated. The machine whirred. The machine presented me with two twenties and a tenner. 'Score!' I said.

I grabbed the banknotes. And they were real. Papery and crispy with numbers and the Queen's head. And I shoved them into my pocket. Beth slid her arm through mine like we were married or something.

'I got paid,' I said. 'How should we spend it?'

'Let's go into town!' said Beth. 'Let's go into the city! Let's buy ice cream. Expensive ice cream with cherries and chocolate flakes and the works. And coffee too. And we can walk about and laugh at tourists. And do things people with money do. And then buy even more ice cream.'

I didn't want to be a buzzkill but I reminded Beth we only had fifty pounds and I was planning on giving her twenty pounds' sponsorship out of that.

'How about we just go to a park?' I said. 'Money isn't everything. We could sit on the grass and watch people pass. We don't need to spend money to have a good time.'

Me and Beth, we looked at each other and after about five seconds we burst out laughing.

'Do you want a burger?' said Beth. 'Let's buy a burger. Or there's Mexican street food on the Southbank.'

I had no idea what street food was and, if anything, it sounded dodgy, but she looked at me with a face full of joy, so much joy I didn't know what to do but laugh again. And she started laughing too. And we were standing outside an estate agent's at the far edges of south-east London and we were laughing until tears ran down our cheeks. Well, almost anyway.

'I'm sorry I burnt down your house,' I said, ready to stop laughing.

Beth rubbed my back and said it was faulty wiring and we carried on laughing.

I finally stopped laughing to say I'd better message

Mum if we were going into town because she'd get proper ratty otherwise. But a burger sounded like the best idea ever. Or whatever she wanted. But a burger. I love chilli burgers. Did she love chilli burgers?

'I love chilli burgers,' said Beth.

And as we waited for the bus to take us to the train station to take us to London to take us to expensive ice creams and chilli burgers, I took a photo of Beth and me, hiding my chin with my left hand as I did so. I posted it to Facebook, my fingers tingling, the first time I'd posted anything for months. It appeared in a stream of other people's holidays and I thought that if the summer had taught me anything about life, it was that anything could happen. Anything at all.

Even Beth could happen.

'I want it to stay the last day of the holidays forever,' I said.

'Shut up,' said Beth and grabbed my arm and hugged me. I think she thought I was being romantic. What I actually meant was I still hadn't finished my History coursework.

But that could wait.